Brothers from Another Mother

Walter McAuliffe, Christina Romeo

WARNING:

Not recommended for reading on a toilet. Side effects may result in laughing until you pee, having the crap scared out of you, and/or constipation resulting from the aggravation in the pages ahead.

Contents

About the authors

Walter McAuliffe lives in New Jersey, but he could live, thrive, and survive just about anywhere. McAuliffe was on his own for much of his early years. A slightly off-spec soul and blessed with a sense of humor, the good Lord chuckled, then dropped McAuliffe into the river of life without a flotation device. Watching him being carried downstream, he shouted a blessing, "Good luck and keep the Faith!"

Like everything else, raising yourself has an upside and a downside. You are free to live life without being micromanaged by a family unit. However, when reality replaces family, the result is a lot of missteps and hard lessons that are never forgotten. McAuliffe views life through a different prism; he often rationalizes and functions differently than his peers. Is that a positive or negative way to go through life? If asked, he'll respond, "Rule number one, life is not fair."

Walter is a screenwriter and the author of *Impossible Apostles*, available on Amazon.

***

Christina Romeo is a devoted Licensed Clinical Social Worker who earned her Master's in Social Work from Ramapo College. With a focus on working with marginalized and vulnerable populations, Christina is committed to promoting acceptance, diversity, and self-worth. She firmly believes that self-awareness and self-acceptance are essential to personal growth and healing.

A chance meeting marked the beginning of an unexpected friendship and a path to healing. Christina met Walter, a Vietnam veteran seeking support. Walter found that Christina understood his unique perspective and genuinely believed what others failed to acknowledge. Their bond, built on mutual respect and the therapeutic power of storytelling, allowed Walter to share his stories and history, finding healing and purpose in the process. This profound connection inspired the co-creation of their book.

Christina's dedication to addressing life's complexities is evident in her writing and clinical practice. Her journey with Walter highlights her belief in the transformative power of storytelling and personal growth. This commitment to connection and compassion defines her approach to fostering healing and authenticity.

Prologue

"Go on, be honest, you walked into work one day and had the unfortunate luck to get stuck with a handi-crapped bed bug...of all the things you could do in this world and you choose to work with veterans- - Vietnam veterans no less! Maybe we should get you checked out by the doc."- Walter

***

A Note from the Therapist:

***

So, you want the truth? I'll tell you how it happened. I work as a clinical social worker in a private practice run by a wonderful neuropsychiatrist. I walked into work on a September morning and stopped by the boss' office to say a quick good morning before getting into a full day of sessions. We exchanged the usual pleasantries, and just before heading out, he said, "I've got a new client for you." There was an ever-so-subtle hesitation. "I'm not sure it's going to be a fit; he's a veteran." I must have given a puzzled look because he clarified, "a

Vietnam vet." I still couldn't grasp why this was *different*. The boss chuckled a little and said, "Just give him a call and let me know if you can take the case."

I spend a few days brushing up on my Vietnam knowledge before giving this new client a call. I dialed the number, told him who I was, and asked to set an appointment for the following Wednesday. I offered him an 8 am slot, and I'll never forget his response, "Young lady, that warms the cockles of an old man's heart!"

8 am on Wednesday came. At 7:42 am, in walked Walter, complete with a cane and as I was soon to learn, a lifetime of *grumpiness* (one of Walter's favorite words). Most clients wait for me to ask the questions during our first meeting. With Walter, however, this was not the case. It was clear that Walter had been to countless initial intakes over the years. He was familiar with the standard questions care providers ask. "Where were you and when were you there?" was always one of the first, followed by a complete list of all his medical conditions incurred as a result of being in Vietnam. I was starting to understand that Walter's experience with other providers was not all that positive and almost always ended in him being more frustrated and grumpy than when he entered.

Despite his previous experiences, I found that Walter was eager to share and did so with a clever sense of humor, a well-crafted defense mechanism that he began cultivating at an early age. During Walter's first session, he took me on a meandering journey through his career, marriage, and subsequently his initial interaction with the Department of Veteran Affairs (VA). During that first meeting, I remember laughing... a lot. Surprisingly, as I was sitting across from a man in obvious physical pain and presumably just as much emotional pain. I soon learned that Walter was on a mission to improve his overall health. He was determined to ditch the cane, lose some weight, and hopefully be less affected by everyday triggers that got in his way.

This is where we began our work. I don't claim to be a world-renowned psychotherapist or researcher. What I do claim, however, is a passion for understanding people and assisting them on their individual journeys to improving their circumstances. Within an hour, I was committed to Walter's healing (even if I wasn't sure how we were going to get there!).

Over the next several sessions, Walter and I talked about his PTSD and the ways in which he was affected in daily life. What I discovered was a unique presentation of how his trauma showed up. You see, Walter is a storyteller, and I underestimated this quality as simply being part of his personality. Many of these stories swirled around a central theme: *history always repeats itself.*

Walter spent years, decades in fact, defending himself and trying to prove what, quite frankly, was always in plain sight. Here was the key to Walter's healing. It was so simple. I believed him.

That belief, combined with Walter's love of sharing stories and history, was how this book came to be. I began having Walter write weekly as part of his treatment and it started to help! I began to see a shift in Walter and after a few months of writing, he asked if I would assist in publishing the work he had been doing. I was honored.

What stands before you is a man's collection of stories from a lifetime of lessons, friendships, and the hard times as well. They changed my life, and perhaps they will do the same for you. -Christina Romeo

Introduction

Throughout history, society rested on a bedrock of family (tribe), religion, and country. Pick any era, Neanderthal, Cro-Magnon, Aboriginal, BC, AD, Medieval, or Native, and you will find they all shared similar priorities to protect family, show respect to some form of deity, and to increase the odds of survival through partnership with like-minded individuals. If one cares to look at these extinct societies, they offer a millennium of proven life lessons from which insight, deterrents, and enlightenment can be gained.

Today, we discount and disregard the past; forgotten is a primary canon of existence: "history always repeats itself." The world now worships a digital reality, young and unproven by comparison. Today, *modern man* eats his fast food in the slow lane, and when time comes for a *dirt nap*, he is *erased* from memory. Computer programmers endlessly tap away at the fabric of our existence.

The following fictitious yarn follows a single soul orphaned in a world long gone. Left to raise himself as best he could, he did what was necessary to survive. A natural product of his environment, his personality traits lean toward utilizing history, simplicity, honesty, and sarcasm to solve problems. He has a plain vanilla view on life: "to err is human, but if you really want to screw it up, buy a computer." Considered a foreign concept by today's standards, his attitude is abrasive to many; they refer to him as a dinosaur on an island.

Fighting to persist in the real world, he leans heavily on self-reliance, experience gleaned through hard times, a complete distrust of authority, loyalty to a few proven friends, and a most unusual patchwork of family. He refuses to be a victim of life's circumstances and intends to go down swinging. Nestled deep in the arms of brutal reality, he has taken some hits and landed a few.

Even those who support him find his life bewildering. He does not e-mail, text, Zoom, Facebook, Instagram, print, copy, comment, snap, tweet, FaceTime, emoji, forward, save, or store anything. To him, a cloud is where rain comes from. A true blasphemer, he chooses to exist as a human being!

Giggle if you must, and snicker if you will, but perhaps you should put down your state-of-the-art mobile device. Reflect on where the stress in your life originates. After all is said and done, you both cohabit the same reality. In his world, the current situation is a "big f—king problem!" However, the virtual world deems it to be a "minor issue."

Prior to a fight, a reporter asked heavyweight boxer Mike Tyson, "Your opponent has a plan, does that concern you?" Mr. Tyson replied, "Everyone has a plan until they're punched in the mouth." Somewhere in Washington, D.C., a programmer, high on weed, is about to delete your social security number. Surprise, you no longer exist! The only transactions left between you and your government are the reimbursement of your student loan and a death tax. Be happy, don't worry, government computers will automatically transfer both payments.

It may be time for you to stop playing video games and exit your mother's basement. Is it too late? You'll have to read the book to find out. Why yes, Thad you can download it onto your tablet. Too busy?

No problem, have a flash drive placed in your coffin along with both "proof of payment" printouts.

***

Welcome to brutal reality.

Chapter One

EARLY LIFE LESSONS

*E*rr...no, I did not see Sky King, Roy Rogers, or Andy's Gang this week. You have a color TV. Well, I guess that's good for you...congratulations. Me? I read the paper. Why? It has the want ads and racing form. No, Bruce, they are not new shows. - Walter

***

An old wood-frame apartment couldn't be home, at best, a dwelling situated on a two-lane main road, reflecting limits far beyond money. It was void of affection, joy, and optimism.

Its location ensured a car or two could pass, breaking the mind-numbing boredom of another hot, humid summer night. If the wind blew in the right direction, the fragrance of the DPW's settling ponds would drift down, adding to the nuance. Some say "home is where the heart is." Technically, this was home, but in my heart, I was certain there had to be something better.

In addition to the ample indifference, anger, despair, and jealousy, there were the mounds of pigeon dung in the attic resulting from decades of open windows. I thought of it as "icing on the cake."

There was no need for a clock; the cooler air made it clear it was around 11:00 p.m., time to go to work. My parents were separated, and the old man wanted help with the rent. With her and both older brothers gone, he was experiencing some temporary financial difficulty. A temporary but serious situation, he might even have to cut back on his three packs of cigarettes a day!

I was the only life form left in the apartment. However, the legal age to acquire working papers was sixteen, which posed a problem. The law was intended to protect against child labor abuse. My father, always a cautious man, had to improvise. He reasoned that if his son was never paid a salary, then he could not possibly break any employment laws.

So, when he approached a neighbor to offer my services, the terms of payment were cash only, payable to him. If asked why the money went to him, he would respond, "I put all his money in the college fund; he wants to study medicine. You know how kids are, he would only waste it on baseball cards and candy." You must give the old man credit, he had more angles than a pool shark, and I admit, I liked candy.

Naturally, the fee for each service was negotiable. Picking up old lady Large's weekly suppositories costs less than cutting Milliotti's lawn. For the neighborly milkman with aging legs, he negotiated three nights a week, from Thursday to Saturday, from 11:00 p.m. to 5:00 a.m. He reasoned the hours were viable since school began after 8:00 a.m., and the remaining Sunday evening (so far) was mine. I settled into the weekly rhythm, assuming that's how all fourth graders spent their weekends.

I started down the rickety rear staircase, careful not to use the handrails, eliminating any possibility for splinters. At the bottom, I hopped over the decaying brick stairs and into the parking lot.

It was a short walk over to Don Hall's house. I could see through the kitchen window that Don was kissing his wife and infant son goodbye. We climbed into his car and headed for the garage that housed *Pine Ridge Dairies'* delivery trucks.

The Dairy had thirty-plus identical, small white, bulldog-nosed milk trucks. Ugly and slow, each had one seat and dual controls, allowing the driver to drive while sitting or standing.

Each driver was given a route and acted as a distributor for the dairy. He would buy dairy products wholesale and sell them at retail. Due to their special design, the dairy provided the trucks. No returns were allowed, and any breakage (all bottles were glass) was his problem. All products, including cheese, eggs, milk, orange juice, cottage cheese, etc., not sold within the expiration date, were deducted from his profit. In effect, each driver ran a small dairy retail business out of his truck.

Don's business skills were almost as bad as his driving. So, my night started early, and I made most of my money illegally from recapping dairy products with a new "sell by" date. As the only one in the garage too young to prosecute, I took on this task for all the drivers. Young but street-wise for my age, I kept my mouth shut and was paid accordingly. When finished, I returned the re-cappers to their hiding place behind the garage's large ice machine.

The old man knew what I was paid to deliver milk. However, he had no idea how profitable recapping could be. He would never know, since Don and the other drivers could be terminated if word got out. The next chore was to load the truck and shovel mounds of ice onto everything. Ice in large quantities countered the aging of some products in the heat and humidity of summer nights. Finally, the drivers came together, sharing profanity, cigar smoke, and slightly wet pink and white forms. After the garage manager's review, the doors were opened, and they headed out in a cloud of smoke.

The behavior of their delivery men balanced the unsurpassed quality of Pine Ridge Dairy products. Don was typical: *get the crap off the truck* as fast as possible with minimum effort. The margins of his route book were covered in milkman shorthand. Each page was painstakingly printed with a needlepoint pencil. Even as the small truck bounced along cobblestone streets, the crisp ledgers were easily read with the help of a tiny dashboard bulb. The vertical monetary margin carried unpaid balances from Wednesday, Don's collection day. If you were behind in payments, you got recapped milk. At the bottom of the page, he very lightly, ensuring easy erasure, entered details on tonight's delivery.

The top horizontal margin outlined directions in unique "milkman's shorthand," quickly guiding the little truck from stop to stop. It served as the forerunner of today's GPS systems. Our rate of delivery was further enhanced by the late hour, absence of traffic, and Don's total disregard for traffic lights of any color, one-way street signs, or blinking danger warnings.

Hudson County was comprised of cities, boroughs, and towns that were not blessed with affluence. Don, based upon his work record, was assigned a majority of poor, crime-ridden neighborhoods. The kind local police patrolled with a minimum of two officers per car. Naturally, there were no walking patrols. They parked just outside these neighborhoods, between 1:00 a.m. and 4:00 a.m.

Always a wave and a smile for us as our truck rambled by, heading deep into a world most people never see. They bet on whether Don and I could get in and out unscathed. There is a reason why people say "it was as different as night and day." Perhaps they spent a night working on a milk truck in the slums.

All milk was sold in one-quart glass bottles. The milk carriers were stainless steel and held twelve quarts. Based upon rampant theft, customers insisted that their delivery instructions be adhered to. Milk was left in hallways, milk boxes, on window sills, or placed directly in the refrigerator. Every milk box, house, apartment, and ice box had a lock on it.

Carrying twelve quarts and rings of keys up and down endless five-story walk-ups, while keeping your pants from sliding off, was exhausting. Reading handwritten notes scribbled by immigrants, holding the key rings in order, opening and closing locks, and returning empties was equally grueling. As the night wore on, you felt your knees go first, then your back, and finally, your legs cramped. No time for a break; the clock was an evil taskmaster. I was paid $5 for the short route and $7 for the long one. But I received $20 a night for half an hour of sitting down recapping milk. Some say, Crime doesn't pay?

Under fringe benefits, there was a free education in the lessons of life. I learned what it meant to be homeless, along with lessons in alcoholism, drug addiction, wife beating, and prostitution. Each night, the bars in Hudson County closed at 2:00 a.m. as required by law. By 2:00 a.m., Don was usually parked in front of Shirley's diner on 35th Street. This was the milkman's lunch hour. While Don ate, I ran the store. To his credit, he usually returned and gave me a small coffee with a buttered roll.

Regardless of season or weather conditions, I was left in the truck to keep an eye on its contents. Milk trucks are equipped with a small heater that occasionally works, but they lack air conditioning. Given the hour with the bars closed, my clientele mainly consisted of prostitutes. Almost every one of them purchased chocolate milk. Young and naïve, I assumed it was for self-consumption. Older and wiser, I now realize it was purchased for their children. The 1950s were a different time; convenience stores were still decades away, and legalized abortion was not even discussed. Lucky for me, or I would not be writing this.

Even in the worst neighborhoods, a milk truck could be found on the way home. As time passed, I became familiar with many of the neighborhood ladies and developed a respect for them. They made the best of the "cards they were dealt" and fulfilled their responsibilities as single parents. In addition, they thought I was cute and often tipped me. Their generosity, when added to the recapping money, covered me for the upcoming week.

Don never knew, so my old man never knew.

Unfortunately, a typical night had ugly situations too. It was not unusual, when entering an apartment lobby or climbing stairs toward a landing, to run into one of life's unique and dynamic individuals. Stairwells were tight, and these lost souls could not be avoided. When the hallway's low-wattage lightbulb was working, I could avoid the bottle, needle, feces, vomit, and urine. They knew I didn't carry cash. Confrontations were avoided by acknowledging their existence and showing them a token of respect. Usually, a simple "Good evening, boss, sorry to disturb you," would do.

One year, Dad had a close encounter and was almost exposed to a judgmental society. Unknown to him, Friday's homework assignment included an essay entitled, "How did you spend your weekend?" The following Sunday, with my best #2 pencil in hand, I outlined, in detail, my milk runs from that Friday and Saturday night. The title I chose for my manuscript was "All prostitutes Like Chocolate Milk." I handed it in on Monday, figuring it would at least earn a B+, and never gave it a second thought.

***

Early Tuesday morning, my home room teacher, Sister Dennis, was standing over my desk, stuttering and shaking. I was hauled into the principal's office.

My old man was already in the office, facing a mix of concerned religious faculty. All were eager to hear his explanation as to how one of their fourth graders could write such an accurate paper describing a drug, alcohol, and sex filled weekend. God bless him. Completely blindsided, the old man got on a roll and never looked back. Without hesitation, he threw me under the bus. I was surprised to learn I had undergone a drastic change stemming from desertion by my mother. Dad was at his wits' end trying his best to raise me as a good boy. On weekends, he arranged for a babysitter so that he could attend church functions. Obviously, he was shocked to learn what the sitter exposed me to.

I said nothing because I was utterly baffled. Every line in my essay was true and reflected personal experience. How did an old milkman suddenly become a babysitter? Dad squeaked by and quickly left the office. From then on, I was forbidden to hand in any homework without his permission.

During a frigid week in January, I headed for Don's house to begin another working weekend.

Mrs. Hall answered the door and explained, "Don left. He couldn't take the grind anymore."

That Wednesday, he headed south along with all the payments collected from his customers. On his way out, he added the contents of the dairy's safe. Don had gone from milkman to embezzler in just one day.

Once again, brutal reality touched my life. Still worse was the fear and concern on his young wife's face as she juggled their child, closing the door on my first job. What the old timers say is true: "all you have left are the memories."

Go figure.

Chapter Two

BIRDS OF A FEATHER

Your mom said not to hang out with me? No, I don't have to go home when the street lights come on. I don't understand why the street lights are dangerous? No, I don't play Little League, that takes time, and I work. Yeah, that's right I work. Eh...no, Chas, work is not like Little League. To this very day, I am still suspicious of street lights. -Walter

***

Suburbia dominated America in the 1950s. Early rock 'n' roll gave way to the Beatles and the Rolling Stones. TV shows *like Leave It to Beaver* and *Father Knows Best* gave children and their parents a look at how society viewed the ideal family. Well-mannered housewives were the norm, divorce was rare, crime was low, and politicians were considered "honorable." It was a different time when honest simplicity resulted, to a great extent, in a stress-free lifestyle.

The 1950s kaleidoscope of problems, be it religious, social, medical, political, criminal, mental, etc., co-existed in complete concert with daily life. However, there was no Internet, and 24-hour news programming did not exist. The cumulative result was that fewer people had knowledge of society's ills. People invested their time in their job and family.

I wish I could have experienced that type of life. Honest, I do. Since my parents were separated, the 1950s Catholic soft speak for divorced, and many of my jobs were not legal, it was not to be. My hard-boiled employers had already taught me about politicians and religious leaders in great depth. They taught lessons in brutal reality and things unknown to kings.

Of course, all relevant lab work was performed on the street. When a problem arose, it was discussed and dealt with. This was long before the *concern* for someone's feelings and the use of soft speak. In this timeframe, a serious issue was referred to as a big f---ing problem! Politically correct speech was nonexistent. Conversations were held in a colorful, succinct language that left little room for any misunderstanding.

I was living a more mature lifestyle. What I said and how I acted made other parents nervous. In addition, I was living on about $12 a week during a time when the average kid's allowance was less than $1. I could tell when someone tried to blow smoke up my ass, and I spoke to adults as if they were my peers. They found that to be alarming.

My income was hard-earned and tax-free. In addition, school was free, and dad provided a dry bed and food (sort of). But he fell short on the required clothing and personal hygiene. For example, during this time, hair was worn short, and Dad considered the cost of a buzz cut to be a significant investment. I was forced to take a few fashion risks.

Half a century ago, most couples married for life. If they had children, they accepted responsibility to support them at least until they reached adulthood. I shit you not! If a catastrophe struck, the extended family shouldered the added responsibility of support where they could. The child support network we have today, of school breakfast, school lunch, after-school activities, weekend dads, weekend moms, daycare, and all the rest, did not exist.

My situation was rare for this day and age. When Tommy asked, "Mom, he's here, can I go out and play with him?"

His mom replied, "No, stay away from him. He looks like a bum."

So, birds of a feather led me to a strange collection of childhood friends. Boys my age from single-parent families were scarce. We found ourselves in a society that did not recognize us because we were a tiny percentage. We were on our own. Friends became family, and we figured things out together. I was very mature for my age and acted accordingly.

Spread over two towns, seven of us managed to find each other. Before high school graduation, long before the creation of mobile phones, several of us would already have *cell numbers*. Steadfast and loyal to a fault, we considered each other to be a "brother from another mother." We leaned hard on each other to make it. Our friendships that formed when we were off balance, under stress, and constantly being challenged grew into robust relationships. For over half a century, they have remained rock solid.

Chapter Three

BIG FRANK

*D*id you hear? Timmy's dad brought him a new bike. I guess that's good for Timmy. A birthday party down at the bowling alley? Sorry, I have to work on Saturday. But hey, thanks for the invite... it's appreciated. -Walter

***

Big Frank Brunlotti ran B&F grocery, a typical neighborhood Bodega in Harlem. In addition, he shared ownership of the hardware store next door. Big Frank's son, Little Frankie, and I were best friends and attended the same Catholic grammar school. Since I seldom had reason to go home, I spent a lot of time at Little Frankie's house.

After many years, the family finally got tired of falling over me, and I was accepted as Frankie's half-ass adopted brother. As the years passed, fewer things were whispered around me. Eventually, I went on vacations with the family, enjoying their boat, summer beach house, winter cabin, New York City, and suburban New Jersey homes. It was a sweet deal. I had nothing, but Little Frankie had everything, and he shared it all.

In return, I helped him cheat his way from grade four through eight. Also, because Little Frankie had a speech impediment, I would cold cock those who poked fun at his Italian/English vocabulary. Big Frank did not want his son to have any trouble with the police. He made it very clear that I, on the other hand, was expendable.

Frankie dated any girl he wanted, causing friction with the other boys. My function was to explain to them that Mary Jane preferred to date the boy carrying $200 in pocket money, and in 1950s suburbia, that boy was not one of us.

On the rare occasion that talking failed, things would follow a natural progression of pushing, shoving, cursing, and fighting. After all, I had a lot more on the line than a giggling pile of estrogen. My newfound quality of life was at stake.

I mentioned to Frankie that my career in dairy products had ended abruptly. Without hesitation, he told me his father needed help in his Harlem stores on weekends. No problem, I just had to be at his house by 4:30 a.m. on Saturday. Since I was only in the sixth grade and New Jersey would not provide working papers until I was sixteen, it was a no-brainer.

My   father   wanted   his rent.

After leaving the Bronx market and pulling up to B&F grocery, I began to realize why Little Frankie was well paid. Frank opened the door to a dirty, dimly lit, vermin-infested grocery store. He took us into the kitchen and explained what my new career in retail sales would entail.

Then he told me, "Keep them the hell out of here. I don't care how, just do it. I have to work the back door and the basement. I don't have time for f-----g grocery customers!"

The back door was located at the far end of the kitchen. Made of thick reinforced steel, it seemed suitable for use as a water-tight door on a submarine. The stairs leading to the basement were located out of sight, deep in the kitchen. Whatever and whoever Big Frank let in the back door quickly disappeared down those stairs.

B&F was a combination front and hideout. Stolen goods and people needing a night's sleep on paper bag beds passed through the back door. Business was good, and B&F was open fifteen hours a day, seven days a week. There was a large hole in the basement wall between the two buildings. Well-hidden behind the bag racks, it allowed goods and people to pass between the hardware and grocery store. The NYPD never showed up with search warrants for both addresses.

Twelve years old, and I had already moved on from being a small-time dairy embezzler to working for Frank. The work was not physically demanding, and the weekly pay was fantastic. My pockets jingled full of money. Catholic grammar school girls with their rolled skirts, saddle shoes, and bobby socks were of little interest. They had no way of knowing I spent my weekends serving prostitutes. I prepared gourmet stale sandwiches and vintage warm Yoo-Hoo. If you had the financial resources, special-order chocolate milk was available.

Several times a day, Frank would hand me a cardboard box full of "groceries." The delivery address was written on a small piece of adding machine paper.

His instructions were always succinct and repetitive: "deliver these, eat the address, don't look in the box. After you're paid, leave the building through a different door than the one you entered and bring me the cash."

I learned that "fresh produce" was costly. Living on them seemed like a great way to diet; I found it weird how Frank's select inventory made his customers so thin.

When asked, I told my old man that I delivered groceries to the needy in Harlem. He got his expected seven dollars, then told me he was proud of what I was doing and hurried out to purchase another carton of Camels. I kept almost all my pay while receiving a doctorate in 'Urban Slum Lifestyle'.

Like any job, there was a downside. I was an unarmed twelve-year-old white boy walking around a black ghetto carrying either "fresh produce" or money. Still, the neighborhood knew who I worked for and what was in the boxes. It was rare for Little Frankie or me to lose any money. In those instances, Frank would be remarkably calm and wanted a description and location. He would contact his customers, inquire as to a name and address, and then a co-worker would eventually collect Frank's money.

To help keep the neighborhood *bed bugs* away, he pinned a huge yellow and black button on us. It depicted a black silhouette on a yellow background that proclaimed, "I love Big Daddy." Big Daddy was the local evangelist wrapped in a bed sheet. He preached from a third-floor fire escape on Saturday mornings. His deacons would walk the street collecting money from the adoring crowd. Frank told us always to make the same contribution; five dollars was a respectable amount in the 1960s. Baptism was only held on Sunday since they required turning on a fire hydrant and finding a hose. The white kids holding five dollars got wet on Sundays.

To this very day, I wonder to what extent Big Daddy played in keeping me out of harm's way. Perhaps he performed weekly miracles on my behalf. Each of us worships our own invisible man or woman in the sky, and others no one. Lesson learned, Voodoo to Hindu simply respect each other's preference and move on.

Along with the deliveries, Little Frankie and I were responsible for managing the grocery store. To assist us in keeping customers out of the store, Frank never plugged in the soda machine, and the resultant warm water was never changed. So, each long-necked bottle of Yoo-Hoo "imitation chocolate drink" (That's right no f---ing chocolate) sat in filthy warm water with grunge around its neck. Little Frankie and I were sure no kid would consider drinking it. The damn things sold like cheap cold beer on a hot summer day!

To make matters worse, the local factory workers kept coming in for lunch sandwiches. Believe me, Frank was not happy! However, he was a man of action. The cold cuts, except for bologna, went into the garbage along with all the bread and butter in the kitchen. Frank returned and placed a can of 10-weight Texaco motor oil on the grill. He had a brown bag of what appeared to be pigeon food, one-to two-day-old broken hard rolls. The new menu consisted of either egg or bologna, fried in pre-heated Texaco motor oil, on a two-day-old roll. A warm Yoo-Hoo was optional. Still, sales remained brisk, resulting in great distress.

One Saturday, two young men confronted little Frankie at the counter. They expressed displeasure with the fare being offered. One requested a refund while tapping his stiletto on the counter. Frankie told him he would check with the chef and assured him that immediate action would be taken. As usual, Frank had prepared Frankie well in advance for how to react.

A tapestry of obscenities flowed out of the kitchen, followed in short order by Big Frank. He walked to the front door, locked it, and spun the open sign to closed. As Frank pulled the front shades down, two of the largest human beings on earth stepped out of the kitchen.

They began to explain how rude it was to pull a knife in Frank's store and made indelible impressions on the head and body of each man. All left via the back door. I saw one exit with an open switchblade handle sticking out of his rear pants pocket. Just the handle, I could only assume where the blade went.

The commute in and out of New York City left time for conversation. As Frank took sips from a bottle of Seagram's 7, he would teach us about the real America. By that, I mean politicians, corrupt politicians, and the absence of non-corrupt politicians. I learned many *things not taught to kings.*

Frank's lessons served me well throughout my life. His description of a politician is as accurate today as it was back in the 1950s. He warned me, "if you are walking down the street on a bright sunny day, the guy who walks up to you, simultaneously looks deep into your eyes while vigorously shaking your hand in both of his, trying earnestly to convince you it's raining out while he goes *golfing, pisses,* on your shoes is no doubt a politician."

Frank was trying to convey the similarities between the mob and the government. Bless the old mobster, he not only sheltered, fed, and paid me, but Frank also gave me an early awareness to judge things realistically, not emotionally. The wide chasm between these two philosophies confused a sixth grader. The history book and religious teachings leaned one way while brutal reality taught another. Great Americans created the Constitution and the Bill of Rights. Yet, most of the founding fathers condoned slavery. God is all-knowing and all-seeing, but is God not good with money? That made no sense to Frank. He reasoned that anyone "all knowing" could make a fortune at the horse track. Why do we have to take up another collection for him every week?

I worked for Big Frank for several years. He was a worker bee well outside the center of power. The work spanned very long hours, sometimes in dangerous situations, with zero margins for error. Frank lived in a harsh world, and it happened that one Sunday, he went missing for a couple of days. The police finally found him at the bottom of a ravine in upstate New York. When questioned as to why he was in the ravine, he replied, "I went for a walk."

They also asked him why he was carrying five thousand dollars, to which he responded, "I was going to buy a Sunday newspaper."

A quiet man, he said little. So, when he spoke, everyone listened carefully. He was of medium height with a thick, solid body like a walking bulldozer. All his movements were rapid; if you walked with Frank, you soon found yourself jogging.

Big Frank was far from perfect, but I owe him an awful lot. I am sure the brutal life lessons he taught me were influential in my getting out of Vietnam alive. Many more perfect souls did not.

Frank locked the storefront and climbed into the huge Pontiac station wagon. He looked at me and said, "Irish, I've got to stop on the way home and make a pick up. When I stop, you get out, head for the corner, and wait for the lady. Give her this brown envelope and take the bag."

He caught me by surprise; we never stopped heading home before. I asked, "Frankie is riding shotgun, wouldn't it be easier for him to slide out?"

"No," he replied. "When she shows, look at me. I will give you the OK, but if I turn on the lights, start the car, or motion you off, bring the envelope back to me."

I was streetwise but still very young with a lot to learn. As we drove, I rolled the situation around in my mind. "It was back ass-ward. We always delivered the 'groceries' and came back with the money." Although I was never made to feel it, this was in part why the family adopted me. As before, when necessary, I would take the risk while Frankie and his dad watched. The wagon slowed, and Big Frank parked near the corner.

Here I am, a 14-year-old white kid standing on a corner in Harlem around 11:00 p.m. on a Friday night holding a fat envelope. *Now what?*

I saw her step down from the apartment staircase. She was well fed, well dressed and well spoken. "Shit, this is sweet. A small white kid," she said in the form of a greeting. "No way I could miss you. Is that envelope for me?"

When I turned, Big Frank was already showing the thumbs up.

"Maybe, what have you got for me?" I asked.

"Your box is coming; it will be here in a minute." Then she re-marked, "You know, a white boy standing on the corner holding an envelope full of money is not too smart. Do you want me to hold that for you?"

"No," I said. *Now at least I knew what was in the envelope.*

A car pulled up, the window went down, and out came a box. I took the box; she took the envelope and got in the car. *Batta-Bing,* as the slang goes, a few seconds at best. I wasn't that fast, but I hustled back to the station wagon. In an instant, Big Frank had his jungle cruiser rumbling toward the George Washington Bridge. I noticed he never looked in the box, and remembered the young lady never looked in the envelope. Whatever type of transaction just took place, the buyer and seller trusted each other.

Once back in Jersey, instead of home, he headed toward the Turn-pike and parts south. It was obvious Frank was in a bad mood. Frankie never asked why, and neither did I. We headed south in silence just under the legal speed limit. Frank found his exit and headed straight for an all-night fast-food hamburger joint. He pulled into the dri-ve-thru lane and stopped at the talking clown. Boffo sputtered to life and asked, "Can I help you?"

Big Frank replied, "Yeah, I wanna know what kind of meat is in your chicken nuggets?"

Annoyed, the clown asked, "Who the fuck are you?"

Frank spoke loudly and slowly into the clown, "Give me a name, who the fuck is running this shit hole?" The clown face went silent, its speaker hissing.

Then a deeper, older voice said, "We use Australian spring lamb."

Frank put the station wagon in gear, rolling up to an already open window, the box passed hands. He paused for a second and stared hard at the manager and growled, "We need to have a chat, you ain't goanna like it." Gunning the Pontiac, we left, driving North on the Turnpike well above the speed limit.

Little Frankie filled in the dots for me. Many drug users purchased their product at a fast-food window. The family owned a commercial bakery contracted to supply hamburger rolls to the restaurant chains. Early each morning, fresh rolls in large plastic trays are stacked high alongside the kitchen door. Deliveries are made quietly and safely all night long before the stores open. Most trays are red in color, except for a few blue ones. Rolls in blue trays contained the "special" of the day.

All you need is one employee per restaurant working the window and "customers" who know how to order a "special." The result was by far the largest chain operation in the state. It ran around the clock with no overhead. If one found themselves in front of a judge, all they would have to say is, "Your honor, what more can I say? My client went to a respected restaurant chain to buy what they advertise, a hamburger."

Brilliant.

Chapter Four

SECOND HAND SON

D o I want to come over and play? Can I come in time to watch the Mickey Mouse Club? Darleen and Annette wear amazing sweaters which hide massive protrusions of some kind. -Walter

***

I was sixteen and legally employed packing and shipping books. Well, almost sixteen, I didn't *outright* lie on the application. I was just a little confused about my exact birth year. Finally, I had a legitimate job. I could now experience indoor employment with no life-threatening overtones and reasonable hours (sort of). Twelve to fifteen hours a day lifting freight consisting of forty-to sixty-pound boxes of books.

Now that I was earning, the American political system reached out and touched me. Before I ever saw my first paycheck, the politicians grabbed their percentages. Legal employment certainly had a downside! If society considered Frank to be a mobster, no suitable adjectives exist to describe those thieving bastards properly! The lesson learned on this job was that people who lift books all day seldom have the intellect, time, and or energy to read one.

Mom was long gone, but on the upside, Dad finally had sufficient child income to keep him in Camel cigarettes, coffee, and gasoline for the entire summer. Finally, he received "a legitimate taxable" income on a regular basis. Each Saturday, I would leave his rent on the kitchen table. Happy as a clam, he left me alone; we seldom crossed paths that summer.

For the first time, I was a member of the national workforce and experienced the difficulties of marginal jobs. The benefit of taking a late lunch was easy to recognize. From time to time, when pulling a pallet from deep in the bowels of the warehouse, I came across a foreman or some level of supervisor trading *bodily fluids* with a co-worker. My early years of providing dairy services and sandwiches to prostitutes prepared me well for these "warehouse lust" encounters. I would quietly keep working while ignoring the amazing body contortions demanded by rough sex performed on a shipping pallet. I was certain the pay increase (hush money) would come in time, and it always did.

The years spanning 1950 through 1960 were transition years for American women. The equal rights advocates came up short, and the amendment was never ratified in enough states to become the law of the land. Women did not receive equal pay or promotion consideration in the workplace. However, in divorce court, they lost their previously long-standing default as to child custody. Divorce settlements, alimony, and those who received it were in transition. In the process, the "stay-at-home mom" was disparaged. Society gave us the working mom and the single mother. The young single moms humping boxes (pun intended) were *victims of life's circumstances*. They were doing what they had to do in a fast-changing society. They provided for their children in the absence of a deadbeat divorced husband. Many received no family support and were blindsided by the new normal.

Toiling in a shipping warehouse provided an excellent vantage point from which to analyze the urban poor in the 1960s. The interface between alcohol, drugs, and unemployment became clear. As addictions wore on, showing up for the minimum required six consecutive months of employment became increasingly impossible. Those few who made it were eligible for a fresh six months of unemployment. However, most were doomed not to complete the next cycle.

Education was clearly one of the few ways out of a dead-end job. In addition, the military, religious orders, and gambling were all possibilities. It amazed me how those most affected had disdain for both education and their boss. They never considered that after a year or two of school, they could be the boss. A fundamental concept, such as doing their job correctly, instead of marginally, would result in a wage increase, which was deemed by them a foolish prospect.

Like all things in life, picking and packing freight was a learned skill. The worst, back-breaking orders, usually in a bookstore, entailed placing loose books into various-sized boxes, sealing them, and then lifting hundreds of loose boxes onto pallets. Each box had to be lifted into the proper position to stabilize the pallet load, like building a stone wall by hand. Fitting just one box correctly might require several lifts. In sharp contrast were orders for hundreds of the same book. These orders were standard and usually generated by a college or school district. When multiples of the same author and title were ordered, the books were pre-boxed and palletized by the printing house. The packer stamped the "ship to" on each pallet.

Because God has a sense of humor and life is not fair, all orders were picked, checked, and then dropped by forklift onto the packing floor. White lines painted on the warehouse floor established the pecking order for all shipments; first in, first out, and shipping lanes ran left to right. A working lane must be empty before moving to the next lane. Orders were placed front to back in the lanes after they were checked.

Sounds simple. The manager, who had arranged numerous meetings to discuss the creation of this procedure ad nauseam, was unaware of reality. While this "meeting room wizard" ate his favorite donut and drank fresh coffee, he created a cluster f—k! He forgot rule #1, life is not fair. Stir in a little of life's brutal reality and watch the fun begin! Each packer had an employee number, and his productivity was based solely on the number of boxes sent for shipment. Period.

So was his continued employment and any consideration for a wage increase.

The foreman with an IQ lower than a Martian soil sample had enough trouble just counting the boxes. Absolutely no consideration was given to the degree of difficulty incurred in preparing an order for shipment. Polite established rules for the orderly retrieval of sequential orders from shipping lanes, but they were blown by faster than shit through a goose.

Summer was the busy season, stretching the workday from 8:00 a.m. to 9:30 p.m. The warehouse floor was noisy, hot, and humid. Fork truck exhaust fumes mingled with those from the trailer trucks. Add to the misery, a social dynamic spanning two extremes. Local high school kids working a summer job on their way to college, and year-round employees from the inner city. Both wanted the same thing: to make the foreman's count with minimum effort.

In this corner, Chris: 19 years old, father of one, two-timer on parole, recovering addict in poor health, taking it one day at a time. In the opposite corner: Harry, 16 years old, strong, single, and carefree. It is 3:00 p.m. on Friday, and both are tired, covered in sweat, both with their eye on the same easy order. As they moved toward the front pallet, upon which nestles the shipping paperwork, Chris looked around before pulling his box cutter. Since he has nothing to gain, Harry backed off. If the foreman terminated Harry, it only means more time on the beach with the bon-bon beauties. Chris, on the other hand, had to support his family and (on occasion) his habit.

Unfortunately for Chris, I also needed the job. He had no way of knowing my situation or that I was a graduate of Big Frank's Harlem school. In addition, he was unaware of my time working the inner city "great unwashed" milk route. What he did learn was that there was one white kid who appeared to know how to handle himself and where to stand with a box cutter. The same kid grabbed and held shipping papers on choice orders before they reached the packing floor. The summer marched on. Chris spread the word to his friends, and I watched my ass.

Eventually, based solely on performance (*no, life is not fair*), I was promoted and trained to drive a forklift. Months later, while dropping orders, I noticed Chris took to wearing long-sleeve t-shirts. As time passed, he would miss a few days of work each week. Later, caught high on the job, he was terminated.

Chris and I were not that different; we raised ourselves and needed to earn a living. In hindsight, I had one significant advantage: Catholic school. Catholic schools were very different than public schools because they did not *have* to teach you. Expulsion at any time, with no repercussions, was their option. Heavily disciplined for over twelve years, I was better prepared to absorb the disappointment and unfairness.

Chapter Five

MORAL COMPASS

*G*eorge Carlin *summed it up in his stand-up comedy show.* "*Who's coming? Jesus?*" *No shit! Quick, look busy!*" *- Walter*

***

I owe a tremendous debt to the nuns and priests who provided me with an excellent education and a moral compass—a debt I can never repay. In the ignorance of youth, I could not recognize, much less appreciate, all their work. In my defense, it was done in a manner a boy could easily take for granted. They were surrogate parents providing patience, direction, comfort, and when necessary, discipline. The typical class size for one nun was forty-five students. In my class, seven of us were considered potentially marginal.

It was my senior year in high school. The switchboard in the convent closed at 10:00 p.m. Every Friday, Saturday, and Sunday at 10:00 p.m., the nun working the board would call my old man and ask him if he knew where I was. He found that to be highly abrasive, since he never knew how to answer. I disliked the calls even more than he did because every Monday, I had to account for my weekend. Finally, the good sisters decided that monitoring my behavior was not working.

I was invited to attend interfaith dinners on Saturday evenings. Since I was a charity case, supported by the generosity of the parish, all my Saturday evenings were spent in a convent. A positive byproduct was the respect I learned for people of all faiths.

***

My finances were getting lean; Dad was still getting my pay for the milk runs. As a result, recapping milk became my sole source of income. Meals at the corner diner, haircuts, and toiletries were strictly cash and carry. Since young ladies on a date did not pay for anything, hunger and celibacy were becoming old friends.

Larry and I were close, all the way back to kindergarten. Like the rest of us, he came from a single-parent family. This was unusual for the time; his mother supported him and two siblings. Just like the rest of us, Larry was broke, hungry, and looking for love. He and I often served as altar boys at the weekday 6:00 mass.

Larry knew I was struggling, and while waiting for the priest to arrive, he asked, "I have an idea to make easy money, do you want in on it?"

"Of course," I replied, "What are you thinking?"

He laid it out. "Look he said, every morning we get here well before the priest. That little refrigerator in the corner stores sacramental wine. I know where they hide the key; second drawer from the left, in the back, on the left."

I opened the drawer and there it was, right where he said it would be. "Great, but it won't work; only a matter of time until someone walks in and catches us drinking."

Larry looked at me, put his arm around me, and said, "Oh yee of little faith have I ever forsaken you!" What he said next even surprised me, "Saturday between masses, I took the key and had Max's hardware make a duplicate. Be here tomorrow, half an hour before mass, and leave the thermos in your lunch box empty. We should get a quarter a pop." Just like that, the gang was in a very profitable bootlegging operation.

Weather permitting, after lunch, open-air recess was held in the church parking lot, which served as a playground. The guys would find an open spot along the perimeter out of earshot. Topics discussed ranged from weekend plans to sports and girls.

Across the street, inside the church, the sacrament of confession was offered to parishioners in need. The telltale sign is a line of old women clutching their Bibles, waiting for their turn. After a lifetime of breaking balls, these "ladies" were hoping to negotiate a better deal with their God.

That gave Larry an idea. There were hundreds of kids in that parking lot, and all of them had lunch money. We listened as he made his pitch. "Each sin against God results in a different penalty. Why not take bets on what penance applies to a specific offense? The bigger your offense, the more prayers and good works you had to complete before you attained forgiveness. Instead of ten horses like a race track, we would offer ten prayer sets or timeframes. For example, a bet would be on the total amount of applicable prayers in ten prayer increments from 0 to 100."

After much discussion, the guys finally agreed to an interesting wager. "What is the penalty for screwing a giraffe?" Five to one odds on giraffe intercourse seemed appropriate. Starting, the action was limited to boys only, but instantly, the girls wanted in. Evidently, they had an even bigger interest in penalties for bad behavior (who knew!) The gambling took off. Inquiring minds wanted to know the consequences for bad behavior.

Pip, Dip, Mickey, Larry, and I acted as runners. All ten-cent bets were funneled through Rob. Using his sharpest No. 2 pencil, he faithfully recorded the action in his composition notebook. Meanwhile, Luke acted as our lookout.

In a short time, our "clientele" pressed us for additional betting opportunities. Pip suggested a new bet, and it immediately became a popular wager. "What does a cannibal get for eating someone?" The motion was adopted at three to one, and the bets flooded in.

Then our new venture, just like all our ventures, ran into serious problems. Somehow, we had to produce a certifiable winner for both the giraffe and cannibal wagering. The only person with the answers was ordained and sitting in the church. There was no way around it; someone had to ask him. We pulled names, and I lost. Mickey drew the Cannibal wager.

The next day, during lunch break, I got in line with the old ladies. That's when Sister Thomas noticed me. Now the good sisters were already suspicious. It seems the bootlegging had some mothers concerned about their son's new fondness for breath mints. We had no way of knowing the wine was ordered every month.

So, no matter how carefully we siphoned off each bottle, a massive increase in consumption was clearly visible. Either all the clergy had become winos or there was mischief going on. It was easy for the nuns to narrow down the source of the higher demand; It was the rectory, certainly not the convent! Still, they had to approach the pastor cautiously. The good father was a bit miffed and advised them, in the rectory, that all wine was kept under lock and key. Say what you want about Larry, he was good. He was perfect! As usual, the sisters began interrogating the upperclassmen about missing wine. It was fun to watch them wilt under pressure. However, things were getting hot, and we limited our bootlegging to only trusted customers. Thankfully, our latest venture, the gambling ring, was not even on their radar.

On her way to the playground, Sister Thomas spotted me. She made a detour in my direction and inquired, "Master Walter, what are you doing in line?"

"Waiting to go to confession," I replied with my most angelic smile. She wasn't buying it. But what were her options? The old ladies were watching, and it would look irreverent to pull me off the line. Smacking an angelic young boy on a confession line was not viable. She got in the line, turned with her back to the women, and gave me the stink eye.

Through gritted teeth, she said, "You hurry back on the playground when finished."

I smiled and replied, "Yes, sister."

The curtain was drawn, and I was sitting in a dark confessional, beginning to wonder if what I was doing was a good idea; why piss off God? I prayed daily and often felt that he was the only one covering my ass. The little window slid open; it was speak now or bail on the guys. "God dammit," I blurted out. "Bless me, Father, I have sinned. I screwed a giraffe." I anxiously waited for a response, but heard nothing, just silence. Minutes can seem like hours.

Then the pastor's voice, calm and measured, came through the tiny opening, "Walter, I want you to leave the church and think about your behavior."

"How the hell did he know my name?!" That trick was limited to God or Santa, and December was still a long way off?!

In a stupor, I said, "Jesus! No, wait, I didn't mean that! I don't know what I mean. Sorry, I'm leaving right now." As I opened the curtain, I stammered, "So, what exactly is my penance?" In the complete absence of any response, I decided it was time to leave.

Walking back to the playground, I considered my options. We were being pressured for answers by gamblers, each sure they had won. If I told the guys what happened, they would insist I keep trying. One thing I was sure of was that there was no way I was going back to poke God again. It would be easier to bullshit the guys. As soon as I reached the playground, they were on me like a wolf on a meat truck.

"What happened?" asked Larry.

"What did you find out?" Pip asked.

I told them, "They gave me two weeks of helping the nuns; you know the usual, clapping erasers, and picking up trash on the playground."

Mickey wanted to know if I had to say prayers.

"Of course," I replied. "They gave me forty long ones." *What was with him and the details?* I told him, "Hey, if you don't believe me, you go ask." Tomorrow it would be his turn; let him get a dose. Nobody cut me any slack. Next time I went to confession, I was undoubtedly going to ask what the penalty was for pissing God off.

The following day at lunch, Dip told me he heard the pastor was asking around if anyone in the parish had a pet giraffe! I was stunned and exclaimed, "Jesus Christ! No, wait, I didn't say that. God damn! No, no, I don't mean that either!"

Dip asked, "What the hell is wrong with you?"

"Nothing, just leave me alone," I replied.

He looked at my face, opened his lunch box, and handed me his thermos. "Here, take a hit," he said.

That morning, I opened my fair share of lunch boxes. At the bell, I shoved a handful of peppermints in my mouth and did the bourbon drunk shuffle back to class. It was then that I realized I had to pee. Since recess was barely over, permission to leave the classroom was denied. Sister Thomas shouted, "Master Walter! Stop squirming and sit still." Now, God may work in mysterious ways, but there was no mystery about my intense discomfort.

The grammar school Principal, Sister Rose, spoke. "Pay attention, boys and girls, we have a guest speaker. Brother Jeremiah from the Mary Knolls missionaries is here, and he has come to speak with you boys about a vocation."

From the back of the classroom, someone shouted, "Yo, yo Frankie, you got vacation homes, right? Maybe your dad could hire this guy to clean pools?"

"Silence!" Screamed the short, rotund nun as she banged her yard stick first on my desk, then on me! It hurt, it always hurt. Obviously, God confused Rose with a major league cleanup batter. He blessed her with amazing arms and wrist action; no one had an inside fastball that Rose could not hit.

Missionaries often toil in third-world countries, enduring serious hardship while helping the indigenous population. The work is demanding, and their health usually suffers. Jeremiah was an exception; he was a large man and easily filled the classroom. It had been some time since he had gone hungry or thirsty.

That impressed me since I was leaning hard on the Corner Diner for my sustenance. Dad was not big on meals. Depression, chain smoking, and mounting debt had reduced him to about a hundred and thirty pounds. A typical summer dinner consisted of soda crackers broken up in a glass of milk. In the bathroom, several cockroaches committed suicide and hung themselves with dental floss. Times were harder than usual.

I knew that one way of telling how a man was doing was to look at his shoes. Jeremiah was wearing new shoes (never resoled), polished and soft. On his head, he wore a large brimmed hat, which matched his spotless, pure white cotton robe. A large crucifix and rosary bead set served as a belt. True, a fashion risk in 1960, but it was all tailored to fit, clean, and pressed. I, on the other hand, looked like I fell off the south end of a northbound freight.

Jeremiah spoke, "Have any of you thought about becoming a Mary Knolls missionary? We have missions throughout the world helping people in poor countries. We are having a retreat at our new seminary in Vineland. I invite anyone who wants to learn more about the work we do to spend the weekend with us. To help you better understand our order, I brought along a short movie about the missions."

Then, with a click and short *whirr*, the 8mm projector was happily humming away. The movie was a hard sell, enough to melt the heart of the most ardent atheist. Full of puppies, kittens, and happy children. It droned on for ten minutes.

Later during recess, I asked the guys if they were going to Vineland. Frankie, Pip, and Luke responded with just a look. Rob spit into his can of Coke, and Mickey started to chuckle.

Rob asked, "Are you fucking crazy?" *So much for peer support*. I saw it differently. I ran it over in my mind: "Three good meals a day, air conditioning, a good mattress, clean bedding, and no lifting. It would be a weekend off from work, far away from the slums. A no-brainer!"

Complete with a paper bag instead of a suitcase and a forged permission slip, I climbed into the back of a luxury station wagon parked in front of the church.

The ride out into the country took about an hour and a half. Along the way, we stopped at St. Mary's to pick up another kid. *Great, we aren't even there yet, and I had competition.* When we arrived at the seminary, I realized there were dozens of boys from all over the state attending Mary Knolls weekend.

Immediately upon arrival, we were directed to our rooms for the weekend. I put some hurry up in my gait, ready to fight for a decent bunk. No need! All the rooms were modern, well-furnished, and spotless! Each bed had a mattress to die for. I was beginning to feel pretty good about my weekend with the Mary Knolls, and yet, it still got better, a hell of a lot better.

The next stop was the cafeteria and lunch. They set up a hot lunch, real meat, two helpings, and a dessert. Stuffed, relaxed, and ready for a snooze, I let my thoughts drift, finding myself comparing the Mary Knolls to Big Frank's organization.

It was then that Father Bob addressed all in attendance. Welcoming remarks and a brief mention of his gladness that we came. It was then that he started in on vocations. First, it was just boring. He buzzed on and on; that's when my rear end fell asleep, a common reaction to molded plastic chairs.

It was time to bail on Father Bob.

He stopped me on my third trip to the dessert table and inquired, "Do you really hear God's call?" Caught with my hands full of double-nut fudge brownies.

I responded, "Eh...no father, but if it makes you feel any better, I sure hear your Olympic-size swimming pool calling me. Yep, no doubt." I quickly excused myself, grabbed a handful of vanilla coconut cookies, and headed down toward the pool. Before leaving the cafeteria, I promised to listen for callings and assured Father Bob that anyone walking on water would have my undivided attention.

I learned the next morning as they threw my paper bag into the station wagon, "It is not nice to fool Father Bob." Imagine, drummed out of the Mary Knolls missionaries after just one day. I can still visualize that huge pool in my dreams.

Naturally, the guys were curious and had questions. Sister Rose also wanted a detailed explanation. That old nun wanted more information than I had to give. I told them exactly what happened. While swimming in the seminary pool, my vocation must have washed off. The one person who could not care less was my old man.

Dad's logic was simple. "Go be a forest ranger, proctologist, monk, hobo, astronaut, or rodeo clown. Be whatever you want. Just be certain to have my money." He was running low on cigarettes and wanted to know where the hell I was all weekend. He was so upset he forgot to ask for money! However, he did ask where the clean bed linen and bath towels came from.

I told him, "I don't know, they just appeared like some kind of miracle."

Go figure.

Chapter Six

BELCHWISERS

*W*hat is the meaning of sex, wine and rock 'n roll? Just follow the
railroad tracks, and you'll find out. – Walter

***

Most of our classmates went to summer camp. Mickey and the rest of us never went to summer camp. For reasons unknown, Mickey was jealous of the campers. He would say through clenched teeth, "I bet they aren't happy!" If you questioned Mickey regarding his backwards logic, he would become agitated.

I, on the other hand, knew they must be pleased, and I was certain every one of them was enjoying their summer vacation. It was always fun to discuss Mickey's bikini-clad girlfriend, who just happened to be on vacation. The guys bantered on about how much fun she must be having sunbathing with all her new friends. He would soar to new heights of anger, and watching him lose control was one way to break the monotony. Any option, including *poking the bear*, was more attractive than humping endless cases of books in a very hot and humid warehouse.

The warehouse was located at the back of an industrial complex bordered by railroad tracks. The rails were hidden from view by thick woods, complete with a stream. After work, the tracks and adjacent rail siding offered a welcome shaded and unencumbered shortcut to the road. As usual, the bunch of us walked together. The conversation continued about Mickey's girlfriend. We would fire off obscene questions like:

"How many depraved sex acts could someone complete in just one night on a remote moonlit beach?"

"What is the correct meaning of orgy?"

"What type of sex toys, lubricants, jellies, and food products such as whipped cream and peanut butter are allowed at orgies?"

"How often do farm animals participate?"

"What exactly are the maximum limits for male and female participants?"

It never took long to achieve the desired effect; Mickey, trembling, had completely lost his mind and babbled vile vulgarities at us while he tried to remain upright on the tracks. Nothing new. We derailed Mickey at least twice a week. Just looking at the poor guy provided the comic relief needed after a long day. Still, we knew when to stop and always did just short of the fist fight. Mickey was loved; he was one of us, and no one wanted to break him.

It was normal to walk past empty box cars on the siding. On this evening, we came across three full box cars. Pip was the first to notice that one car had a partially open door. There, in the soft glow of a summer sunset, we could see box after wooden box of...wine! Wine boxes were stacked on pallets six rows high, and the railcar was stuffed with pallets, front to rear. Imagine the awe, surprise, and indescribable joy that came with the realization that what we were looking at was real! We were teenage boys, no adults in sight, staring at unlimited alcohol, and the entire summer ahead of us to drink it!

The light was fading, but I think Rob experienced his first erection. Pip, teary-eyed, was struggling to increase the door opening. Mickey quietly wet himself. Larry was hopping up and down like a handicapped kangaroo. I was frozen, motionless in a state of serendipity. Dip lost it and was trying to climb over Pip to get into the car.

Luke, always the calm one, started to take control. "Dip you flaming asshole, get off Pip. Larry, Walt, you two keep an eye out for railroad workers. Does anyone have any tools?"

In just a moment, Rob, Pip, and Dip joined Luke in the car. "I have a box cutter," said Rob. A smiling Dip announced he had a pocket knife, complete with a corkscrew.

"Great," said Luke. "Now we need to walk the tracks and find something to pry open a box with." "Walter, search for metal, something heavy." I returned with some old rusted railroad spikes. "These will do," Luke said, "now find a couple of rocks we can use as hammers."

It didn't take long for a case to be opened, followed closely by the first bottle, and then everybody was sitting in the car with their own bottle. The first wine we tasted (guzzled) was a lovely Italian red. For all the guys knew or cared, it could have been a Greenland purple.

The wine soon had its desired effect. A completely contented feeling that comes when one settles into the warm arms of an alcoholic beverage. "Warehouse? Books? What books?"

Pip was having a hard time keeping up with the replacement bottles. Since he alone had a corkscrew, he was, by default, the designated bottle opener. Naturally, opening bottles for others limited his consumption. That was unacceptable, so he stopped opening bottles and sat on the nearest case.

The sun had long set, and it turned pitch black inside the car. Sober only by circumstance, Pip suggested we discuss our newfound fortune. "What do we do with all this wine?"

The first answers coming from the drunken darkness were expected: "We drink it, dummy!"

Other drunken replies followed. "Bathe in it...swim in it... gargle and float face down in it." He expected the response. After all, drunk or sober, his chosen friends always excelled in stupidity!

This time, the lack of maturity irritated him; an entire trainload of wine was at stake. He shouted his next question into the darkness. "Okay, shit heads, finding it was easy, but what now?"

Emerging briefly from the darkness to grab another bottle, Mickey slurred his answer, "What now? Why now, we drink it!" Unhappy with Mickey's problem-solving abilities and inches from his face, Pip growled, "Listen, you dumb son of a bitch, we can lose this wine as fast as we found it!"

Luke squeezed between them, suggesting they both pull up a case and sit down. Since he had consumed voluminous amounts of something red, white, purple, or maybe pink, Luke felt the need to fall on a case near them. Pip turned toward Luke, "Look, anyone walking the tracks can find this same way as we did...and, what about the god damn railroad?! Don't you think they want their railcar back?" Pip was never an "A" student or a "B" student, for that matter. More like a "D" + with some "C's," but he did make a good point. He began to calm himself by consuming copious amounts and quickly became useless. Still, his point hung in the summer air.

Stated, "What happens to the wine, left on the tracks, when tomorrow or the next train arrives?"

Luke came up with the best course of action. The car was on a siding, and we had a whole weekend; our wine was not going anywhere. We would remove the boxes slowly, all night long, and bury them near our homes.

Late that night, those who were still conscious agreed to meet early the next morning at the railcar. The unconscious would have to follow their instincts. Like every other plan we concocted, this one was flawed. The more we drank, the less we could haul away. With my head pounding, I loaded my last load of Dip onto my bike. Since I did not have to hide or bury him, I just dumped him on his front lawn next to the *caution dip* road sign.

That first night, I did not get home until very late. That is, I think I got home, anyway, it was either dark or light out. Luckily for us, we belonged to a small minority of our time (1950s). It was well before the advent of cell phones and the Internet, and coming from single-parent homes, there was little need for teenage supervision. When available, nurturing was invested in younger siblings. The conditioned assumption to explain my absence was that I was working overtime or staying at a friend's house.

The following day, I slept well into the afternoon. I finally got up, dressed, grabbed a gut bomb for lunch, and as promised, I headed straight for the siding. Surprise! All the rail cars were gone!

A passerby saw me crying, concerned, he asked, What's the matter, kid?" Referring to the car, I answered, "She just disappeared, vanished, I don't know where she went or how to find her."

The passerby advised, "Young love is like that kid. Hang in there; it   will pass."

It was time to find Luke and chat about his bullshit planning abilities. Finally, I came across him sitting with Larry on the sidewalk.

They were leaning against the drug store wall. Neither of them looked remotely happy, so I decided to let it go. Besides, it was an especially hot summer afternoon.

As I walked up, an argument about their dire financial situation was escalating. Larry grabbed their last $5 and ran into the drug store, ignoring Luke's loud warnings that "Ice cream melts and soda never stays cold!"

"What's he gonna buy?" I asked.

Luke muttered, "Who knows, this whole day has been a debacle."

Soon, Larry reappeared, grinning broadly. Holding a small paper bag, he asked, "Would you guys like to go swimming, hiking, or horseback riding?"

Luke merely moaned, "What did you blow my last five bucks on?"

"Look," Larry said, shoving a small box of tampons in Luke's face. "Right there on the box: *enjoy swimming, hiking, and horseback riding*. All we have to do is figure out which is which and how they work. My guess is you add water or something."

Luke, unlike Larry, had older sisters. He took a long look at the box, stood up, and punched Larry in the head. Hungover, terribly disappointed, and now broke, they headed home. *Their ship (train) had come in, but the rail siding collapsed.*

As they walked off, I could hear the Beatles singing on Larry's transistor radio, "Christ it ain't easy." Another stinging lesson. Just like young love, wine trains come and go.

Still, it was a summer to remember. Each of us managed to relocate at least several dozen bottles of good quality wine.

Luke (bless him) had another grand plan. He got us to agree to go camping each week: no special reason, just the urge to do what boys do.

Each of us chipped in for a single package of hot dogs that we carried all summer from backyard to backyard. We sharpened some branches, built small fires, and brought blankets. To the untrained eye, it was a harmless evening of Boy Scout wannabes enjoying some summer backyard camping.

The cover worked like a charm; it was one of Luke's best ideas. We learned patience and waited until the younger siblings were called in for their bath and bedtime. This coincided with the sun setting, allowing us to uncork in the welcome darkness quietly. Luke demonstrated how to turn on our blankets sideways, facing the fire, with our backs toward the house. Then drop a straw in your bottle and quietly sip all night. Most of the guys extended their evening with a beer or two. No one's father would ever miss a beer or two since they purchased the stuff by the case. Any sommelier would agree there is nothing like a good bottle of Liebfraumilch washed down by a couple of *belchwisers*. Obviously, the need to eliminate indigestion and bodily fluids resulted in some unusual grass stains (damn grubs)! When the stains appeared to spell out names, the explanations became harder to formulate. The occasional tummy discharge was blamed on slug mucus, and pain caused by indigestion was relieved by a fart lighting contest. When a parent expressed concern about seeing a flickering blue light, we pretended to be clueless. The electric company never found the cause.

Still, there were some close calls. Like the rest of us, Larry suddenly developed headaches resulting from "allergies." The only cure was to sleep late quietly.

One morning, his mother burst into the room, visibly upset, demanding that he follow her into the yard. "Mom, what's wrong?" he asked.

Her response, over and over, was, "Hurry, come quick, I need you."

In a matter of minutes, he found himself in her backyard garden. She whispered, "Be careful. There is a bear or mountain lion around here!"

With his head pounding, he replied, "Mom, that is impossible." She grabbed his arm and pointed to a pile of feces. "Big," she mumbled. "Bigger than a human being!" Squeezing his arm tighter, she asked, "What are we going to do?"

Larry told her, "Mom, don't worry, I'll take care of it."

"When?" she countered.

"Okay, Mom, right now," he answered. Hungover, Luke picked up the phone.

By the time it reached his ear, Larry was already screaming, "Luke, you dopey bastard, why did you pinch a loaf in my mother's tomato patch!"

"What are you talking about?" Luke asked.

"Don't give me that crap, I know you did it," Larry hollered.

"Calm down, Luke pleaded; how do you know it was me?" Larry was adamant, "I'm sure it was you." Luke replied,

"Really, are you some kind of ass detective?"

"Bastard!" That was the last thing he heard before the line went dead.

When an adult became too curious, the *firewall* was always, "Look, Mom, I cannot become an Eagle Scout unless I learn to camp." *Eagle Scout, my ass!* These guys were more like lookouts. In 1950, mothers and most fathers respected Eagle Scouts. Once again, Luke was certainly on top of things.

Another problem was the dozen or so empty wine bottles appearing in garbage cans each week. Confused neighbors suspected many scenarios, ranging from a cheating spouse, delinquent son, drunken relative, or inconsiderate passerby.

Fortunately, the mysterious bottles only appeared every six weeks in random garbage cans, making it hard for the adults to figure out what was going on. The mystery deepened due to the absence of any sale price or outlet markings. The wine we had *captured* was a brand not stocked by local stores.

Just like Larry, Luke was good.

Very good.

Chapter Seven

MRS. MOM

*I*f there is a heaven, I have no doubt Jane Muller (Larry's mom)
arrived by rocket and those running the place immediately got
an earful. I loved her. Long before equal rights for women, 401 Ks,
IRAs, the elimination of sexual harassment, school lunch programs,
after-school programs, food stamps, welfare, and equal pay for women,
she made a good living. Jane fought in a man's world and won. She was
the prototype for the single working Mom of today. At 5'4 and a little
over one hundred pounds, her outward countenance was one of petite
feminism. However, if you were foolish enough to anger her, you'd better
have a first aid kit in your car. Oh, and ice, lots of ice to place on your
private parts. At this point in my life, I had no fear, except for street
lights. However, I had a healthy fear of Jane Muller. -Walter

***

Larry and I lived a mile apart; it was late, dark, and cold. I decided
it was time to get home and was putting on shoes when Mrs. Muller

walked into the kitchen. She looked at me and said, "Walter, I need to talk to you."

Surprised, I straightened up and stammered, "Honest, I didn't do it."

Jane Muller understood tough times and could see through my veneer. She continued looking at me, "Walter, be quiet and sit down. If you'd like, you can stay here tonight. Of course, you'll have to get your father's permission. I can make a bed for you on the sofa." Then, I heard those life-altering words. "Walter, I have decided to leave the kitchen door open for you each night. There will always be a tub of peanut butter and a loaf of bread on the table. If you drink milk, it's in the refrigerator." I just stared at her, unsure how to respond. "Well, are you interested?"

"Really? Sure! Yes! Thanks, that would be great!" And just like that, I had my second family. This time, I had two brothers and a sister, but no father.

Larry became my "brother from another mother." All through high school, Mrs. Muller was true to her word. Soon, I considered myself to be her "second-hand son." That was my term, not hers. She always referred to me as part of her family and never made me feel awkward. On top of her everyday struggles, I am still amazed to this day how she tolerated the added grief and worry we put her through. It was enough to piss off a pope! People say, when all is said and done, all you have left are your memories. Some of us are probably going to wind up in nursing homes. Remembering old times, we will sit in bed and laugh for hours while the attendants check off *dementia*.

We camped several times in her backyard, practicing for our Eagle Scout test. Aside from the tomato patch incident, Jane was unfazed by it all. When Larry suddenly developed allergies, she told him he would just have to tough it out. Allergies were only seasonal, and there was no extra money for a runny nose. If it persisted, she would give him the common remedy for everything in 1959, aspirin and an enema. Now, in 1959, there was no such thing as a "fleet" enema. A spouted ceramic pot was filled with very hot, soapy water. A seven-foot-long rubber hose, complete with a clamp at one end and a curved eight-inch-long perforated plastic bone on the other end, was connected to the pot. The bone was shoved…Eh, *positioned* in the affected orifice. Once the pot was lifted high in the air, the tube became as tight as piano wire. The clamp was released, and the fluid mix, assisted by the massive force of gravity, rushed down through the bone. You could feel the back of your eyes being washed.

No surprise that Larry quickly and firmly declined her prescribed treatment. He was careful to smile when hungover, never again mentioned allergies, and assumed the matter was considered closed. However, Larry had no way of knowing his concerned friends were constantly reminding his mother about his suffering and dropping grades. Bottom line is, he got an enema, and we all laughed our asses off. We heard Mrs. Muller tell him that if he were not any better, she would repeat the procedure the next morning. The guys listening in his kitchen were rolling on the floor. Should you ever face the dilemma of receiving an old-fashioned enema while nursing a head-splitting hangover, I suggest you consult Larry in advance. He is one of only a few surviving experts. He spent the rest of the day nursing a sore ass and sore head. When mom examined him, he would take profound, breaths through his nose in rapid succession. He sounded like an exploding steam locomotive. As a result, Mom left him alone. In the end, Larry was cured of his maladies and enjoyed a spurt of improved test scores. Hey, what are friends for?

When it came to making money, Larry had more angles than a pool shark. It just so happened that there was a pool hall down the street from our high school. Like a one-eyed cat, Larry stood for hours watching the regulars play. One day, he walked in, hung up his coat, paid his three dollars, and racked some balls. A week later, he agreed to bet $5 on a game. He promptly got his ass kicked. Over the following weeks, he lost every bet, depleting his funds and mine.

Walking to his house one day, he explained that the solution was to practice more. After all, "there was big money to be made and all it would take was a little skill."

I heard him out, then asked, "Okay, but you suck at pool, and we are both out of money. How do you pay for lessons and practice games?" He looked at me and, without hesitation, told me he was going to get his own pool table.

"Oh," I said, why didn't I think of that? Eh...just a little curious, how do you intend to pay for one? Plan on selling your unicorn, swindling a Leprechaun, or maybe hustling one of the seven dwarves?"

"No," he said, I'm going to ask mom for the money."

I shared my thoughts, "Well, I would like to be there when you do. Maybe I can help get her foot out of your ass." I tried to reason with him, "Mom works hard and is barely getting by, you can't be serious?"

The following Saturday, Larry called and asked if I would help him load a pool table into his mother's station wagon. I still have no idea where the money came from. My best guess is that he played his ace and called a guilty dad for help. A sensitive issue I deemed best left alone.

Mrs. Muller pulled up the driveway and told us to get that table out of her station wagon; she was in a hurry to leave for work. Larry waved goodbye, and we turned our attention to the vast, heavy box leaning against his house.

In everyone's life, some rain must fall. I saw the dark clouds coming, but decided to wait until Einstein figured it out on his own. To get through the side door of his house, you had to pass through a 4X6 mud room. The room was at a right angle to the door of the house. That's when Einstein hollered, "shit! It ain't gonna fit!"

I sat down on the steps and pondered the Saturday I had just thrown away. Larry stood in the driveway, frozen, crushed. It wasn't long before surprise turned to anger, and he headed for the garage. He emerged with tools and politely told me we were going to take the side off the house.

"Larry, I think that's a bad idea," I said. In a trance, he began to remove the door. In about three hours, we had the side of the house, along with the pool table packaging, strewn down the driveway. The pool table, on the other hand, now sat perfectly and unscratched in the basement where Larry was gleefully racking up. That's when I heard Mrs. Muller come home from work. I was sure this was it. *I was. Going. To. Die.*

Since there were no doors left on her house, she quickly made it downstairs. "Why? What the hell? What are you two? Stupid?" I could see her eyes starting to turn blood red, and her face began to contort, signaling that an evil spirit was being unleashed. I backed up, hoping to put the table between me and her. She was having none of it and began a familiar move. She took off her high heels and, like a baseball pitcher, hit us both in the *lavalier,* dropping us to her level. Now that we were kneeling, she had our attention.

Looking straight into our eyes with her hand under our chins, she told us that the house was going to be put back together, even if it took all night. The driveway was to be spotless. Nothing to drink and no supper until she was satisfied. Larry asked if she would go and buy some nails. He was a brave soul. Stupid but brave. No dice, she was red hot. "Use the same nails you removed."

Larry protested, (It's a miracle he lived through this episode) "Mom, it's dark out, how are we going to find any nails?" Mom dropped our chins and stormed upstairs. Case closed, verdict pronounced, good night, nurse.

We finished somewhere around 4:30 a.m. Every flashlight battery and bulb in the house was drained. We did a good job; the windows and doors were level and plumb, everything was trimmed out, and most of the reused nails were holding. Only a lunatic would wake Mom up at 4:30 a.m.

I told Larry, "I'm going to sleep. You coming?"

"No," he replied, "I think I'll play some pool." Funny thing about lunatics: some play pool.

Like a moth to a flame, the new pool table drew all of us to Larry's basement. As the summer marched on, we spent much of our time enjoying air-conditioned competitions. There was a built-in, well-stocked bar in the basement. Mickey purchased a bartender's manual and began bringing small bottles of mixers with him. Soon, we had regular classes on "the cocktail of the week."

That summer, Mrs. Muller was surprised to see Larry so willing to watch his brother and sister while she went to work. It was entirely out of the norm, and although all her alarms were sounding, she couldn't put her finger on why. Of course, she had good reason to worry, but it would be a few more months before the pieces came together for her.

Mickey was slowly draining her bar stock and replacing it with tap water. Summer ended, as it always does. School opened, and before long, the holidays drew near. Mom invited her co-workers over for a Christmas party and was very surprised to find her guests had nothing to drink. Terribly embarrassed and apologetic, she worked her way through a long night. After saying good night to her last friend, she closed the front door. It was now Larry's turn to experience significant discomfort. Woken from a sound sleep, he tried to focus and make sense of her rant. Slowly, he put two and two together (Like pool, he stunk at math), and his dread began to grow. "It was Mickey and the guys!" he told her. "Get them over here," she snapped! So once again, one of our schemes went astray, *what a surprise!*

Larry, the bastard, played this one smart. He called each of us and said, "Come on over, Mom has a Christmas surprise for you." The gang arrived at the house in no time; we were eager to see what Santa left for us. Pip asked her what she got him.

That's when mom took off and went absolutely bat shit crazy. I thought we had finally pushed her too far, but after a while, she returned to sanity. Each of us would have preferred coal to the reprimand we got that night. Santa certainly defecated in our dream boat that Christmas.

***

In 1965, all the elected officials in New Jersey had a collective brain fart. They decreed that the legal drinking age in New Jersey would become 21 years of age. In essence, they condoned drafting young men at 18 years of age but adjudicated that they were too immature to have a beer. Hmm? In the neighboring state of New York, the legal drinking age remained at 18. Where did all the young men in New Jersey go on weekends?

***

Thankfully, Rob had a car, sort of. It was a black, four-door 1939 Plymouth, complete with big bubble fenders and running boards. From the exterior, it looked like a real jungle cruiser. They say beauty is in the eye of the beholder, and through Rob's eyes this was a Cadillac. He would wash and wax it, the equivalent of painting a white line on a dirt road. Both the speedometer and odometer were broken but based upon the smoke and noise it discharged, we safely assumed the car was well broken in. There were some bright spots; the back seat was more comfortable than a sofa, the interior dome light worked, and one of the headlights worked. None of the windows were damaged, all the doors worked, and three of the four tires held air (slow leak). Still, the broken windshield wipers and defroster triggered some concern.

"Well, you can't have everything. People in hell want ice water." Rob and his Cadillac got us to and from *our* bar in upstate New York. The only bar where several young men could use the same 18-year-old's driver's license if proofed. When it snowed or rained, one of us would lay flat on his back underneath the dashboard. There, he could manually work the windshield wiper linkage back and forth. Another drunk simply sat behind Rob with a rag wiping the inside of his windshield, and two flashlights, wire-wrapped around the front bumper, solved the headlight problem.

Finally, life was good! We had each other, abundant amber liquid, and the money to buy it. A bevy of bonbon beauties frequented both the bar and the back seat of the Plymouth. But like everything else, we hit a metaphorical speed bump. The elected *pant loads* in New Jersey found it extremely abrasive when young men flaunted their new drinking regulations. "My God! The tax loss alone!"

They went back to the sanctity of their governmental chambers and gave birth to a new cluster f---. Every Friday and Saturday night, they would unleash the New Jersey State Police, and they would form a picket line along the border between New York and New Jersey. Healthy fines for drunken driving would restore money to their towns and cities. In effect, what this collection of wasted sperm accomplished was forcing young drinkers, with new driver's licenses, to find poorly lit back roads at night to avoid the police.

One foggy summer night, in a heavy mist, we manned the jungle cruiser and headed for home. Before starting on our covert route, responsibilities were assigned based on sobriety. Luke would operate the wipers while I acted as the windshield defroster. Larry and Pip stood outside on the running boards, listening and looking for other vehicles. Dip looked for flashing lights out the rear window while Mickey, too drunk to help, as usual, warmed the back seat.

Like a Civil War blockade runner, we rolled down the mountains of upstate New York, dancing on back roads and side roads. Apparently, Rob had consumed several adult beverages, and despite his poor driving, thick ground fog, and poor road conditions, we were making record time. Part of our itinerary utilized a new interstate highway that was still under construction. We had sufficient manpower to lift the wooden barricade out of Rob's way and reposition it once through. With a broken gas pedal pressed hard against rotted floorboards, we flew down the modern interstate, safe in the knowledge that police do not patrol closed highways.

As we neared our exit ramp, we noticed a new highway sign prepared for installation. The sign, measuring three and a half feet high by ten feet long, had the name of our town spelled out in reflectors. Drunk or sober, that sign was a once-in-a-lifetime find. Like monkeys trying to screw a football, the guys quickly had it balanced on the fenders, and Rob navigated the jungle cruiser toward Larry's nearby garage. We shoved the sign in and went home for some sleep.

Early the next morning, too early, my phone rang. On the other end of the line, Mrs. Muller, speaking in a controlled tone, said, "Walter, I want you to get the sign out of my garage."

"What sign?" I asked.

She replied, "Walt, I want you to get the sign out of my garage." The line went dead and I realized it was once again *case closed good night nurse*. She was waiting at the garage door as I walked up the driveway. The conversation began with, "I could not go to work this morning. Your sign has my car blocked."

"Honest, Mom, that sign is not mine," I told her.

She replied, "That's not what Larry said."

While I was staring at Larry, she handed me the morning newspaper, pointing to an article on page three. The article explained that defacing a federal highway is not only a federal offense, but it's a felony! Then she said, "You're fortunate. The police are on patrol looking for that sign, and I cannot close the garage door." Larry and I both cringed because at least four feet of reflectors were sticking out of the garage. Her eyes started to turn red, and she growled, "Walter, I want that sign out of my garage!"

After she went into the house, Larry spoke, "I live here for God's sake; there is no way I could have taken the blame for that!"

I fired back, "Call the guys and tell them to get here fast or we are both going to die."

Within the hour, all the guys were in the garage, surprised that, now sober, we could not lift the sign. Luke directed us to go home, "Get all your baseball bats and come back tonight." Once it was dark enough, just like the Egyptians building a pyramid, we positioned the sign on the bats. Then we rolled it onto the little league field behind Larry's house. As we left it leaning on a dugout, we discussed our cover story. We agreed that the little leaguers were out of control, "damn bunch of hooligans!" For the next few weeks, we were all extremely well-behaved while Mrs. Muller calmed down.

Larry's bedroom was an attic dormer, well above the gutters and drain pipes. From this vantage point, one could see the little league field and the tavern beyond it. Also visible was a homeless man named Charlie who slept on the players' bench in the dugout. When given the proper compensation, Charlie would make a trip to the tavern and return with prepaid six packs.

When Larry asked his mom, "Can I have the guys over to play board games in my room?" Mrs. Muller's radar and BS detectors were activated; they were second to none, honed to a fine point due to constant use. Getting beer into Larry's room was accomplished by taking a string, hidden under his bed, attaching a bowling shoe bag, and pulling up a few cans at a time. If we heard noise in either stairwell, the cans were dropped out the window. The designated bowling bag loader always arrived a little late and apologized to Mom.

Just like everything else we did, we were about to run into unforeseen problems. As the empties began to build up in the gutters and drains, water backed up into the house. Mom hired a local roofer to correct the problem before the next storm. She was quoted the usual $35 price to clean gutters and left to go shopping. Imagine her surprise when she returned and was presented with a bill for $200. Naturally, she protested, cried foul, and refused to pay. The roofer calmly walked her over to his pickup truck and pointed to a bed full of empty beer cans. He explained, "I had to disassemble and reassemble all the drain pipes on the house. Then, he told her, "Cleaning eighty feet of gutters was even more fun."

Hearing this conversation from a safe distance, I decided it was time to bail on Larry. "Nope, no way I was taking the blame for this one!" He nailed me to the cross with the road sign routine. Payback is a bitch.

Larry was playing pool in the basement, and I was out the door. By the way, Larry never did play pool worth a damn.

When I got home, Dad told me, "Mrs. Muller called, she wants you to call her back."

"No way, never again!" My gonads and rear end were still sore. I called all the guys and told them to get over to Larry's house. We were taking collective blame for this debacle. I promised to cold cock anyone who did not show; they knew it was not debatable.

They laughed and asked, "How can you be afraid of an old lady?"

To which I replied, "The same way deep-sea divers are afraid of old sharks." Jane Muller scared the bejesus out of me.

I waited down the block until everyone arrived, then, like the sheriff in an old western movie, we slowly walked down the street. Mom cornered Larry and the rest of us in her kitchen, asking, "Why? What is wrong with all of you? I mean, don't you ever stop?"

I had seen this before. The bait was in the water and the shark was circling. Looking at the guys, I went mute and noticed Larry did the same.

Mickey, being naïve, spoke first, "We are...." as his mouth began to form the word sorry, he felt his left ear being pulled and sharp pain from a smack on the right side of his head.

Mom hollered, "Apologies are cheap, but clean gutters cost $200! What are you going to do about that smart guy?"

The following week, our combined pay, along with a non-negotiable add-on for aggravation, went directly to mom. Larry changed rooms with his brother, and the guys considered going to church. Once again, we kept a low profile and stayed quiet. Even the deaf felt sorry for us. Mom, bless her, had to deal with the cards life dealt and seldom had time to remain angry.

If you are fortunate enough to meet someone who loves you despite your behavior and shortcomings, consider yourself blessed. In today's world, there are only a few human beings left. I hope the good lord allocates one of them to you. I lost contact with Jane Muller for almost fifteen years. When Larry called me to advise me that her health was failing, I questioned whether I should call her. Growing up, I placed an added load on her. With a failing heart, the last thing she needed was a surprise call from me! Larry got back and said, "Mom wants to talk to you."

She answered the phone, and I asked, "Mom, this is Walter, your *second-hand son.* Do you remember me?"

Her quick response was, "Yes, I remember you. Always a worry but never anything mean-spirited." The lady summed up my entire childhood in one sentence. Mrs. Muller exited this world not too long after our conversation. Like a trapeze artist without a safety net, I now live life knowing an essential part of me is missing.

Chapter Eight

DYING SLOWLY

P *lease God, before my work is done, bless my life and grant me one good friend. Rob did not die quickly from enemy fire. Quite the opposite, he died slowly of cancer resulting from three years of exposure to Agent Orange. To this very day, his fellow Americans, the President, Congress, Senate, and Supreme Court (the will of the people) deny poisoning him with toxic herbicide and compartmentalize their responsibility. Inflicting genocide on its own Army is a reality too horrific for America to contemplate. Why then has the Veterans Administration published a list of cancers "presumed" to be the result of service in Vietnam and "preapproved" for compensation? -Walter*

***

In accordance with public law 106-65 and in appreciation of their sacrifice, America has promised her veterans $796 toward funeral expenses (no shit 7..9..6 dollars and zero cents, What a country!). I wonder what Congress allocates in support of illegal immigrants each week? Veterans are promised a 3" by 5" piece of stone with an even smaller plaque denoting their name, branch of service, date of birth, and date of death.

In addition, he or she is entitled to two uniformed personnel present at the grave site. They are there to guarantee the veteran basic military honors, fold his flag, play taps, and ensure a dignified burial.

I was embarrassed by the way America said goodbye to my friend and fellow veteran. The United States Navy should be embarrassed, too. Instead of the often-televised pomp and ceremony performed when a President or Politician dies, the US Navy assigned Rob two young men who confused his funeral with an audition for the movie *Top Gun*. I seriously doubt they could fold their socks, let alone an American flag.

Perhaps they suffered impaired vision from wearing aviator sunglasses on a dark, cloudy day? Who knew Tom Cruise designed the Navy's dress uniform? Instead of a sailor playing taps on a trumpet, our Navy produced a "boom box with dead batteries." Rob gave his country four years of dedicated service. In return, his fellow Americans bestowed upon him an unmilitary-style side show performance in front of his mourning family.

He was entombed in a large multi-story mausoleum constructed on the cemetery's northern border next to the interstate highway. Like placing a letter in a post office box, his coffin was neatly slid into an upper repository, the one closest to the interstate. Now for eternity, Rob listens to tractor-trailers downshift around a steep, curved hill. Son of a bitch, some things can make a grown man cry.

I was adjusting to kindergarten, getting a handle on how the place was run. Every morning, a wooden case full of milk was delivered into the classroom and placed on a small table near the radiator (where else?). Give or take, ten o'clock was "rest time." All my classmates lay on mats placed on the floor. It was an opportunity for the teacher to leave the room and for me to drink some milk. I sat under the table reaching up for small containers of moo juice. Very young, I never connected the empty milk cartons left under the table with the kindness of those who let me have them.

I met Rob for the first time while sitting under the table. "What are you doing?" he asked.

"Getting milk, do you want some?" I replied.

His face wrinkled up and he told me, "You can't do that!"

I said, "Sure, I can watch," and I reached for another. Rob gave me his "shame on you, stare," and I replied with an indifferent grin. It has been said that opposites attract. From that morning on, Rob and I remained close friends for over half a century.

We walked down the path of life side by side, always being careful to stick to our side of the path. Rob was a friendly, trusting, and giving soul. In contrast, I might become your friend in a few years, and trust would follow decades later. He continuously opened up my life to new experiences. Things I would never have known without him. In return, I covered his ass and kept the bed bugs from taking advantage of him.

His mother died before he was nine, and his sister, suffering from cerebral palsy, followed not long after. An older brother was on active duty in the Navy. Rob's father had a quiet, strong personality and worked long hours supervising landscaping crews around the state. Although he made a good living, the family's resources weren't boundless, and he knew leaving young Rob alone for days was not a viable option.

Rob was sent out of state to a boarding school.... sort of. His new school was integral to a monastery. The same guy who laughed at me when I was thrown out of the Mary Knolls Missionaries was now a monk! Turns out God has one hell of a sense of humor.

The guys would get together on weekends and then drive out to visit Rob, and he would meet us in his monk get-up, complete with robe and sandals. If the weather was uncooperative, we met in his little monk cave/room thing.

As time passed, it was apparent that the monks were giving Rob regular doses of their Jell-O. The result was enduring religious beliefs and his unwavering devotion to the Blessed Virgin. Both served him well throughout his life. What the monks had no way of knowing was that Rob spent several years with us, consuming beer and wine.

In addition, we introduced him to the Patcharella sisters, Janis with the wooden leg and Crystal with the glass eye. At his tender age, I do not doubt that both sisters took Rob to heaven more than once.

Unfortunately for Rob, that left him struggling with a terrible predicament. Celibacy or ecstasy, pray or drink, what is one to do? We knew what Rob was going to do at least a whole semester before he did. Hell, he would have come home the next day, but he had to address his father's justified concerns. The final resolution was his promise to be very well behaved, improve his education by enrolling in the local high school honor program, and acquire at least a part-time job.

To help you fully understand the forces at work, many years later Rob's aircraft carrier sailed into Subic Bay in the Philippines. The kind of port where penicillin sprints out of the infirmary and jumps off before a ship can dock.

On shore leave, he was in a men's room and while draining his lizard, entered into conversation with the sailor next to him. His new neighbor asked, "You have a New Jersey accent, are you from Jersey?"

"Yes," Rob replied.

Then the sailor next door asked, "Do you know the Patcharella sisters?" Unbelievable, several years after high school and ten thousand miles from home, both sailors still had fond memories of Janis with her wooden leg and Crystal with the glass eye. The monks never had a chance.

During one cruise, his carrier became crippled due to critical maintenance problems and was ordered to enter Tokyo Bay for emergency repairs. The order was unprecedented because American carriers sailed with nuclear weapons on board. As a result, they were strictly forbidden from entering Japanese ports; a directive anyone familiar with WWII can appreciate. Due to the nature of the repairs and the time frame needed to complete them, the captain was directed to get all unnecessary crewmen ashore. If all went well, it would be several days before they could depart Tokyo. As a result, the crew was granted shore leave, providing them a rare opportunity to tour Japan.

So, it followed Rob and a couple of his shipmates who elbowed past angry Japanese demonstrators and began their tour. On active duty, they were required to wear US Navy dress uniforms, and because they were sailors, they headed straight for Tokyo's red-light district. After consuming a voluminous amount of amber liquid and making use of Japan's efficient railway system, they began a tour of the country. In a display of Olympian mental irregularity, they decided to visit the "Atomic Bomb Museum." Why did Rob go to that museum in a United States Navy uniform, knowing the Japanese were angry about his ship anchored in Tokyo Bay? Who the hell knows we're talking about Rob here!

As usual, the museum was jam-packed with Japanese visitors and students on day trips. While looking at murals depicting unparalleled suffering and horrendous devastation, one of Rob's drunken shipmates uttered, in a voice too loud, "Rob, they got what they deserved!"

After the resultant riot, Rob was allowed to familiarize himself with the Japanese authorities. They were gracious enough to provide him with free transportation back to Tokyo and drop kick him back aboard the carrier.

Promptly, Rob and his traveling companions were brought before an irate Captain under tremendous pressure, trapped in an impossible situation. His repairs weren't nearly completed, Japanese demonstrations were growing by the hour, and emotions had reached a new high. The very last thing he needed was the collection of rodeo clowns standing at attention in front of him. Opening with a barrage of demeaning observations about their IQ and maturity, the captain moved on to a vehement and obscene litany regarding their gender, family lineage, and even suggested their mothers were unacquainted with their fathers. He informed Rob that once the ship left port, he would immediately be thrown overboard and used as a shark detector. Rob tried to explain that the situation wasn't his fault. I believe him, but unfortunately, the captain did not.

A caring, sensitive soul, Rob spent his leisure time volunteering to help people in need. So, when Larry's wife called, informing him that Larry was seriously injured on the job, Rob was quick to act. He called the guys together to form a comma watch. Rob and I drew Sunday vigils. After being comatose for a week, Larry's wife was not getting any updates from the attending physician and asked us to inquire about his diagnosis. After advising the hospital staff, both of us minored in premed; we began to ask pointed questions. Due to their workload, the last thing his nurses needed was to be constantly grilled by two jokers. It wasn't long before the lead doctor confronted us.

In the exchange that followed, one thing mentioned by the doctor made an impression on me. Larry's ear had been seriously damaged in the accident. They reattached it but made no effort to restore its natural look.

So, I asked, "Why hasn't the plastic surgeon restored his ear?"

The doctor replied, "If he comes out of the coma, we'll perform the appropriate plastic surgery."

On the ride home, Rob told me, "We need to pray hard for a good outcome."

I answered, "I agree, but perhaps more is called for; this is serious, we need to revisit Larry tonight."

You go to Bargain Booze for a six-pack of that rot-gut beer he loves, and I'll swing by Tony's gut bomb pizzeria. I'll pick up a large can of Sewers Delight pizza with double cheese, double pepperoni, sausage, black olives, onions, and peppers. We'll need a couple of garbage bags, too. "Garbage bags, why do we need garbage bags?" he asked.

I explained, "I'm counting on Tony to provide a real masterpiece." One that will congeal into a pool of grease as the pie cools off on our way to the hospital.

Back at the hospital, we followed the sidewalk lined with flowers on our way to the main entrance. Along the way, we pulled some of the best blooms (damn squirrels) to take to our pal. Once in his room, we discovered that except for Larry and us, the room was empty. We found him limp and asleep in some body harness affixed to the headboard. After putting his flowers in a couple of empty beer cans, we began to administer to our patient.

After extensive consultation and a few beers, we agreed the best method for treating Larry was reactivation of the olfactory, his most powerful sense. Our cure was a delicate procedure entailing the application of gut bomb pizza and rot gut beer; both potent stimulants. We began by whispering derogatory remarks in both ears; then, we slowly alternated the beer and pizza under his nose. In less than fifteen minutes, he began to stir and awakened from his coma. Encouraged, we decided to administer a higher dose of beer and pizza. After inhaling a slice of pizza and guzzling a beer, Larry started to grunt, smack his lips, and wildly slap both hands on the bed and his chest.

"Thank God," Rob said, "You and I have successfully performed a medical miracle."

I replied, "Not bad for a couple of rodeo clowns minoring in premed. Like I told you, Tony's pizza can knock a wolf off a meat truck; hell, I bet it could easily clean out a sewage treatment plant." Just then, the shit, literally, hit the fan.

Larry began to pinch a giant loaf while sitting in bed, so big I thought it had arms and legs. The stench coming from his bed would gag a maggot. Then he leaned over, rested on his harness, and began to emit a low moan while changing color. The aroma must have wafted down the hospital hallway because it wasn't long before a nurse arrived. She looked around the room with a wide-open mouth and asked, "You did not give him pizza and beer, did you? What are you stupid?"

Looking at her, we both followed our instincts and went mute as she continued her rant, "What is wrong with you? Why did you do that?"

In response, I gingerly informed her, "Treating this type of condition is touch-and-go. While attending to our dear friend, an unexpected complication arose. This type of thing is not uncommon in extreme cases."

She pivoted in the doorway and started for the nursing station, providing an opportunity for both of us to head for the elevator.

Riding the elevator, Rob and I reasoned Larry had arisen because we did all the hard lifting. The nursing staff had to change a few bed sheets. It was very unprofessional of her to address us in that manner. Besides, we were highly trained premed specialists, life savers, not candy strippers, what more did she expect from us?

Unfortunately, the accident added to the damage previously sustained in Vietnam, and years would pass before we got him back in the fold. Over time, the guys convinced Larry that Rob and I were responsible for saving his life. He became increasingly appreciative and voiced his gratitude whenever appropriate. However, his family and doctors refuse to see it that way. Apparently, professional jealousy is rampant in the field of medicine.

Just like Big Frank and Jane Muller, Rob's father was instrumental in providing me with family support. The loss of two loved ones, coupled with surviving World War II, resulted in a strong, quiet man. His life lessons were unforgettable because of the method he used. Despite his demanding occupation, he often invited me to dinner.

Being widowed, his dad's meals were served "country style." One evening, the board of fare included broccoli, and I helped myself to some. After tasting broccoli, I (just like most people) decided not to eat it, and to this very day, I dislike eating broccoli. When supper was finished, Rob's dad collected all the plates, scraped any uneaten food onto his plate, and ate every scrap. Just like that, in his unforgettable way, he taught me to be thankful for the generosity of others, appreciate God's bounty, and humbly accept kindness.

On another occasion, a fight broke out while he was at work. One of the guys wound up putting his fist through the kitchen wall. During a rare day off, I watched him repair the hole by creating a small grotto complete with a statue of the Blessed Virgin. As I watched him work, in his unforgettable way, he taught me patience and respect for another man's property.

The man never raised his voice, lashed out in anger, or threatened repercussion. Anyone who judged him to be meek and timid never watched him remove his guns through a ceiling tile in his recreation room. An accomplished hunter, he maintained each rifle spotless and well-oiled, just like the one he carried during WWII. He taught me that when faced with trouble, always use restraint, but when necessary, strike first with overwhelming, never-ending force.

He explained, "Always eliminate the Alpha, the one making loud threats. Surprise him by striking first, and after the other lemmings see you wax his tug boat, they will back off."

Later, if someone shoved me, I quickly responded with a hard swing to the temple. If he bent forward an elbow to the back of his head came next, but if his head went back, a kick in the lavalier followed. Rob's father was a quiet and thoughtful man, but he never forgot lessons learned the hard way in Europe. How could I ever forget him?

Rob inherited most of his dad's attributes, which endeared him to all the guys. He was the only one of us to receive an advanced college degree, and he became an associate professor at the university. On the other hand, I was installing sewerage treatment equipment (Sister Thomas always said, "Master Walter, if you don't shape up, you'll shovel shit for the rest of your life"). A large national company hired Rob as their "Director of Sales Associate Training." The new trainees he taught had to produce, or Rob wasn't going to have the position for long. Since he had no say in the caliber of those hired, it was not long before he found himself in a difficult situation.

In the 1960s, the computerized office concept was still in its infancy. Computer printouts, including those from the accounting and sales departments, were printed on wide, green-tinted tractor paper. Then, I was selling high-end processing equipment. Unlike Rob, I worked from a position of strength with detailed knowledge of my competition, the prices they charged, and every company contact they sold to. Those greenish computer printouts were full of valuable information, including the purchasing contact at each company. Big Frank would have been proud.

Every Sunday afternoon, my young son and I would visit the garbage dumpsters of my competitors. Just in case an unexpected police car pulled into the parking lot, I handed him a tennis ball with instructions to explain that he bounced it and the ball landed in the dumpster. In no time at all, he became an expert "dumpster diver." The weekly and monthly summary printouts outlining company marketing, sales, and accounting were always there for the taking.

Rob was under increasing pressure, and he found it extremely abrasive when I would comment, "How easy it was to sell."

I shared my unique method for sales research, and his jaw dropped open.

Apparently, the university did not offer courses in brutal reality sales. He and his son quickly began bonding on Sundays, and his company sales improved dramatically. They attributed corporate growth to Rob's teaching ability, his academic knowledge, and the high quality of their new sales associates (No shit).

It did not take long before he sensed a slight movement in his moral compass. He asked me, "Walter, is this fair?"

I answered, "Two salesmen will feed their kids tonight; one will eat beans and the other one steak. You do what you want, just don't invite me over for beans."

Opposites attract, resulting in the lifelong friendship we enjoyed. Rob's uneasiness was another example of how different we were. He tried to live an idealistic life, while I felt more comfortable nestled deep in the arms of brutal reality. As time passed, I realized experiencing one with access to the other was an ideal way to live.

The row Rob chose to hoe required him to rationalize and compartmentalize. During a card game, the topic of Vietnam came up, and

Rob elaborated on his experiences as a crewman on board a carrier and his assigned jet. Since the ship never cruised closer than 280 miles off the coast, he reasoned he never hurt anyone. Larry had heard Rob tell his tale before. As a machine gunner with a light infantry brigade, Larry's experiences were coarser.

He asked Rob, "If he knew where the jet he serviced, cleaned, and fueled every night flew during the day."

Rob replied, "I was not involved with flight plans."

Larry's eyes left his cards and focused on Rob. "Let me enlighten you," he replied. "It dropped napalm on towns, fired rockets into small villages, and bombarded enemy positions. We may be going to hell, but you're going there on a jet plane." Just like that, idealism met realism, and the topic never came up again. I understood each point of view. Still, I wish it had never happened.

One curriculum Rob taught at the university was Hotel Management. Students learned how to process and remove accumulated waste products from large properties such as resorts, city hospitals, sports venues, and cruise ships. The approved textbook delved into pollution control, the green environment, respect for Mother Earth, harmony with wildlife, and so forth.

During our weekly screw your neighbor card game, Rob would ask, "You install waste treatment equipment, what are these processing facilities really like?"

My answers did not align with the "approved" textbook.

Rob wanted his students to be well prepared for their chosen profession. So, he went to the administration for permission, and I began to visit his classes as a guest lecturer. When students walked into the lecture hall, they saw a chalkboard outlining the lesson, which read: "**S**olids **H**andling **I**ndustrial **T**echnology." Just the type of learning experience you expect for $200 a credit.

As stated before, my lectures did not align with the approved text-book. Mine covered potable water, water purification, water soften-ers, sewerage, sewerage treatment, garbage removal, red bag waste, and recycling.

We discussed side topics such as: Why do politicians always embez-zle money from the city's solid waste and sewerage allocations? If they are public works, why isn't the public allowed into them? Ten garbage trucks enter the dump; how many turn into the recycling plant? Who do you bribe to rid your facility of asbestos waste?

When the sewerage treatment plant is unable to keep up with the influx of raw sewerage, where does the untreated excess go (should you eat fish the week after Thanksgiving)? Rob's class size began to grow, and the administration assumed the increase stemmed from his teaching ability, coupled with the approved textbook (no shit).

He coupled his experience at the university with his strong religious beliefs and began teaching Sunday school, another way of giving back to the parish. His classes were full of teenage students starting to rebel against authority. Rob expressed his frustration with a few students who constantly disrupted his class, and finally allowed me to attend one.

Unlike mathematics, religious instruction is faith-based, making it easy for the alpha chimps to entertain the class at Rob's expense. The only way to resolve the problem was to interface with the two boys and reduce their class standing.

I removed a ball of twine from my pocket and invited the boys up in front of the class. I asked, "Do you agree that there are invisible forces in your life?" They giggled and responded no, looking at their classmates for effect and support. "What about the existence of good and evil?" I asked. As expected, their response was similar. They accompanied me for a walk down the hallway around the corner of a cross hall. Then I gave them one end of the twine and let it out as I walked back to the classroom. In front of the class, I yanked hard on the twine, shouting up the hall, "Can you see me?"

"No," they hollered. The same scenario followed when asked, "When I stop talking, can you hear, taste, or smell me?"

Back in front of the class, I summarized, "So you two felt yourselves being pulled by something you could not see, smell, or hear." That string simulates what good and evil feel like. Both forces will constantly pull on you during your lifetime. This class teaches you how to live a good life with the help of your classmates and provides examples of how older generations coped with evil." It's your choice, take it or leave it, but I ask you, "Why spoil it for your classmates?" Please take your seats (Rob was watching, so I had to say please).

The combination of losing his mom and sister when very young, being raised by a God fearing and loving father, plus a year of monk Jell-O, produced a good soul. Rob was truly one of the few "human beings" I have ever met in my life. Why the hell did he hang around with us? I'll never know. He enjoyed singing during church services. So naturally, when required to stand, one of us would slide his hymn book down to the other end of the pew. If he made the mistake of putting his offering envelope down, we would take it, and when the usher came with the collection basket, his donation went in as ours. Then, in a voice "just a little too loud" in front of his God, we would berate him as a cheap skate.

At his insistence, we would attend the Christmas celebration at his parish since he was a eucharist minister, and all of us heathens lined up to receive communion from him. Always patient, he endured doses of 'I only eat gluten-free, is this kosher, got any sourdough, do you serve brick oven semolina, and how many toppings?' With the patience of a saint (In hindsight, just like Mrs. Muller, he may have been one), Rob made sure each of us received the sacrament at Christmas without as much as a grimace.

He purchased his home in a small, quaint town and settled into a teaching career. The rear of his home included a large deck surrounded by full-grown oak and maple trees, offering a shady, cool place to spend summer nights with the guys and consume voluminous amounts of amber liquids. Unfortunately, the trees were full of suburban rats, some of whom found comfort in Rob's attic, walls, and on his deck. They chewed through the hose on his gas grill, deck furniture, and table covering while relieving themselves on the deck, railings, chairs, grill, and Rob.

He became so exasperated that he uttered a rare "dammit!" Shocked by that and inebriated, Pip, despite being in a suburban setting, offered to shoot the squirrels.

I told Rob, "I can't think of anything except poisoning the furry little bastards."

Since he had two young children, Rob was disinclined to spread poison and preferred not to shoot, maim, or kill his neighbors. Both suggestions were immediately rejected in an uncalled-for, brisk, and rude manner.

Then Mickey made a suggestion, "Why don't we go squirrel fishing?"

Since none of us knew what he was talking about, Mickey and his suggestion were ignored. Offended he stood up and told Rob he was going down town to buy a pole and bait. When he returned, he had a bag of unsalted peanuts in the shell and a tiny three-foot-long toy fishing pole.

In disdain, he snorted, "Giggle if you must, and snicker if you will. Watch and learn, I'll catch the squirrels."

Then he strode to the backyard fence, where he spread nuts on the ground like fishing boats chumming for marlin. Next, using his pocket knife, he separated the fish hook from the fishing pole line. Finally, he tightly tied the line around one of the peanuts before dropping it into the chum.

As Mickey walked back to the deck, he slowly played out the 2# line from the small plastic reel. Next, he pulled over a lawn chair, grabbed a cold beer from the cooler, and sat down facing the chum. With baseball cap pulled low, sunglasses in place, tiny pole in one hand and beer in the other, he displayed all the intensity of a sport fisherman trolling for swordfish.

After a minute or two, Larry asked him, "What the hell are you doing?"

"Quiet!" replied Mickey, "Don't scare the squirrels."

Rob turned towards Larry and said, "Obviously, he's lost his mind, probably too much discount beer and rancid cheese nips."

"I know he's nuts," Larry said. "But I'm concerned, this is...well, really nuts." Just then, Mickey got a hit off the fence. His rod bent as he cranked on the reel, the squirrel had the nut clenched tightly in its mouth and between both paws!

Thus began the classic struggle between fisherman and fish, I mean squirrel. Mickey was hampered by the limitations of a measly 2# line and a miniature plastic pole. On the other hand, the squirrel was confused and pissed off by an inexplicable, extremely abrasive fighting peanut. The tension built as the timeless struggle between nature and man played out.

At one point, the poor creature was spread out horizontally to the ground. Its rear paws were firmly affixed to the chain link fence while its front paws clenched the nut.

At that point, Mickey cried out, "Skunked! I've lost him, he snapped my line!"

The squirrel scampered up the nearest tree, where no doubt he devoured the offensive legume while planning a bowel movement on Rob's deck. After we apologized to Mickey for distrusting him, Luke was sent downtown to purchase more toy poles and several bags of peanuts. Six lawn chairs were lined up along the deck with beer coolers tactically located along the row. Fishing began in earnest, and a yard full of angry, hungry suburban rats did not disappoint.

A loud, inebriated tapestry of ridicule, excitement, disappointment, and encouragement tinted with just a touch of obscenity rose into the summer sky. Passing neighbors out for their evening walk were stunned by what they heard and saw.

Sweet Jesus, how did this debacle wind up in our neighborhood? My God, what if the kids are watching or listening! What about our property values? Rob's wife was mortified. She turned off the backyard flood lights, emptied each cooler, and gave us the stink eye.

In the end, the squirrels thought they won, but we knew better. Suburban rat fishing became an integral part of all future Drunk-a-thons.

Rob died young from a "presumed" cancer attributed to toxic herbicides, leaving behind a son and a daughter. He had no way of knowing the jet he serviced flew escort for chemical tankers. The same plane he wiped spotless each night.

On a Sunday morning, I visited Rob in the intensive care unit. Arriving too early for visiting hours, I worked my way past the staff and found him in distress. He saw me and, in a very weak voice, asked for help. His large oxygen mask slipped off, and he was having trouble breathing. I was shaken by his appearance, but knew I couldn't show it. Once he was breathing again, I thought about how to break the overwhelming sense of doom hanging in the room. There was a TV on the wall airing a religious program, which gave me an opening.

So, I asked him, "Do you want me to change the channel and look for some soft porn?" He just stared at me, so I continued, "I met with your doctor and he told me your problem stems from too much rough sex."

Still, there was no reaction, so I sat on his bed and made minor adjustments to his full-face oxygen mask. Then I asked him, "How many MIGS did you shoot down today?"

He shook his head and, in a weak voice, told me, "You are endless."

Later that morning, his doctor met with him and his family, advising that there was nothing more they could do. Rob was given the option of going on a respirator or being moved to a private room with 24-hour visiting. God bless him at that moment one of the Lord's best handiworks found comfort in his religion and I watched as they rolled him down the hall to die.

That night, I headed for the hospital to say my goodbyes. Rob was awake, so we had our last conversation even though it was one-sided.

Look, I said, you only get to die once, don't screw this up. If they ask, be sure to deny that you know me and the guys. With your beer gut, ask for a Double X set of wings. If there are options for extra feathers, take them. Don't share your cloud with anyone who chews tobacco."

In a weak voice, he murmured, "You are endless." I kissed him on his forehead and left the room.

Rob died about two hours later, and God got his investment back with interest. Somewhere in the worst of our slums, some kid is looking for help. I have no doubt Rob will answer his prayers.

In the hallway, I ran into some family members. As one would expect, the younger adults were having trouble accepting the situation.

Now I was only a missionary for one day and never a monk, but I had been an altar boy (drunk or not, it counted).

Rob would want me to give it a shot. Drawing on something I heard about Ben Franklin, I tried to recite the story as best I could. Ben was an atheist, but when near the end, he hedged his bet and began to study all the great religions of his time. He concluded that, "We are the product of a kind and benevolent God who places us in a body so we may better enjoy the world he created for us. When the body wears out, bringing us pain instead of pleasure, the same kind and benevolent God returns to remove us from our body."

I am certain the good lord will be extra careful to take your father home in a manner more soothing than sleep.

Chapter Nine

BORN A CENTURY TOO LATE

*H*is father gave him the nickname Pip because that is exactly what he was, "a real Pip." He started out on the straight and narrow, the product of wonderful parents. Quiet and thoughtful, unlike the rest of us, he studied problems before opening his mouth or proceeding to solve them. However, once Pip made up his mind, it was impossible to change it, and that made him a pain in the ass. Even when it was obvious to all that he was dead wrong, he would refuse to discuss it further and clam up. For example, if he decided the world was flat, it was flat, period.
-Walter

***

Pip worked on computers back when programmers dabbled in strange languages such as COBOL, Fortran, and JavaScript. Just the type of work well-suited to his personality.

In the 1960s, programmers were easy to spot; they usually walked around with their fly open and toilet paper stuck to their shoes. His personality also included a caring side, reflected in his studies to become a deacon in his church.

At a young age, under his father's tutelage, he developed expertise in hunting, trapping, and fishing. Pip became an expert with a rifle, proficient in hunting prey at night, and had the patience needed to fish. All traits he would need later in life. His "fellow Americans" bestowed upon him a stint with the 1st Air Cavalry in the highlands of Vietnam.

They took a quiet, gentle introvert and turned him into a young man with problems (issues, to those of you living a virtual existence). Then they sent him home, where his fellow Americans could criminalize and victimize him.

His dad was affectionately referred to as "Mr. B," and just like so many other wonderful people in my life, he allowed me to be "part of his family." As a result, "my stitched together family" now grew to include Pip, his dad, mom, and younger sister.

Due to his position as a supervisor, his only day off from work was Sunday; whenever feasible, he invited me to Sunday breakfast. I enjoyed his company and always looked forward to Sundays with Mr. B.

Sometimes the meal would include fresh game or fish, and I would politely decline. Either way, we sat in his kitchen and discussed what had occurred during the week. Curious in what I had been up to, his questions revolved around school, my part-time job, quality of life, and always "if I needed anything." Unfortunately, my answers were often surprising to him, resulting in indigestion, but he never voiced anger or disappointment toward me. Most of his suggestions carried a little praise, some encouragement, and a whole lot of frustration. A typical exchange went something like, "Walter, did you stay out of trouble this week?"

"Pretty much, one bed bug gave me a hard time, so I gave him a flying lesson."

Mr. B knew that I spoke in my own shorthand, so he asked for a translation. "What do you mean, you gave him a flying lesson?"

"You know," I said. When he wasn't looking, I dropped a few small nails on the back end of his bicycle chain."

You could always tell when the indigestion set in because he would telegraph his bewilderment. After placing his open palm on the back of his neck, he would ever so slowly slide it forward up over his head, then down his face.

Leaning across the table, he said, "Walter, listen to me, you can't do that! Would you like it if he did that to your bike?"

"I don't have a bike, can't afford one," I replied. Bingo, if you listened closely, you could hear him burp.

He was a quiet, strong man who survived World War II. Although he had earned medals of valor, he never spoke of them or the war. Just like other members of "my make-shift family," he was a brutal realist, and just like Pip, he was an expert shot. Every rifle he owned was carefully maintained. While Mr. B wrestled with indigestion, I gained life lessons that kept me out of juvenile detention. I loved him, who wouldn't?

Pip was born a century too late; he found immense pleasure in fishing, hunting, and trapping. His basement resembled a mountain man's cabin circa 1860; animal skins and deer carcasses hung every-where. Once sold, the profit from the furs, along with the venison, was donated to his church. While the rest of us were primed for the high school dance, Pip was wading up and down river banks, setting musk rat and raccoon traps.

It is said that "some people march to the beat of their own drum." If so, our boy had his own band and recording studio. You can find his picture in the dictionary next to individualist. He was fun to be around and too socially involved to be considered a loner, but he was an acquired taste. Naturally, he fit in perfectly with the guys.

One year, during the annual Good Friday card game, he asked me, "Do you like Bourbon?"

"Never had it," I replied.

He produced a bottle of Jack Daniels and said, "This is low proof and very smooth, it will never hurt you." I believed him, it was smooth, and I drank the entire bottle.

A couple of hours later, when my bride came home from church, she found one end of me on the porcelain fixture and the other in the bathroom sink. Exactly the way my "concerned friends" left me. I made it to the bed, and just before I lost consciousness, I listened to Pip rattling his poker chips.

My infuriated bride woke me up after they finally left at 1:30 a.m. She enlightened me regarding the true meaning of Good Friday. While I was trying to stand, she explained, in depth, "Why young children need sleep on holiday weekends." Then she added, "Since you're not much of a father, I asked Pip to take our kids on the Easter egg hunt. If you care at all about our children, it starts at 8:00 a.m. sharp in the town park." Watching me hang onto the dresser, turning green, she was satisfied her last shot had finally broken my gonads.

There were only two choices: I could spend Easter getting crucified by her and her mother, or go on the Easter egg hunt. My head was splitting; it felt like a carnival was going on inside, and the bumper cars kept crashing into the merry-go-round. I considered placing my head where it was ever meant to go; that's when Pip pulled up the driveway on his motorcycle. Naturally, he gunned it a few times for the kids. Sweet Jesus! If I were more mobile, the good Lord would not be the only one who died that week.

After exchanging pleasantries with my bride, the bastard skipped down the street towards the park with a kid on each arm. I crawled after them, starting to appreciate why some murders are warranted. "Uncle Pip" made sure the kids found plenty of plastic eggs. My neighbors watched as I shuffled behind, depositing undigested snacks in their bushes. To this day, my kids remember their Easter with "Uncle Pip." Well, my kids and Jesus may love him, but I don't. God may forgive him, but I never will!

Pip married years after the rest of us, so he could not appreciate the situation he put me in. In fairness, he was an Olympian drinker, something I should have considered. Also, I was aware of the government-mandated codicil in his living will strictly forbidding cremation. The authorities were afraid that once they set fire to Pip, he would never burn out.

After his return from Vietnam, I visited him at home. The conversation was challenging because during his tour of duty with the 1st Air Cavalry, he lost 85% of his hearing. I asked him, "What happened?" He explained that mortar rounds bracketed his bunker. "Dam," I said, "Sorry you lost your hearing."

He replied, "No, it wasn't the mortar; an enemy rocket hit nearby a few minutes later."

"Are you kidding me?" I asked. "

Annoyed, he stared at me and said, "Why would I kid about that?" "Eh...just a little curious, Pip, when the mortar rounds hit, what the hell kept you in the bunker?!"

(Wait for it) "I dooon't knooow," he said. There it was, vintage Pip.

I am sure that everything else left alive in that bunker, including the rats and insects, bolted out in a nanosecond. Once Pip decided to stay, even high explosives couldn't budge him.

Sadly, as one would expect, loss of hearing affected his ability to hunt. One day, he asked, "Do you want to go pheasant hunting?" It was rare for him to invite anyone, so I immediately said 'yes'.

Pip used experienced hunting dogs, and they flushed a lot of birds that morning. Since he could not hear the dogs howling and could not see any birds take flight, he never fired a shot. After an hour of hunting, the exhausted dogs emerged from the thicket. Disgusted with and perplexed by a hunter who didn't shoot, the dogs walked back to the barn. I can't speak dog, but their mumbled growls sure sounded like they were bitching (no pun intended) Pip.

Shortly after arriving home, Pip purchased a brand-new high-performance Chevrolet painted "periwinkle." To pay for the car, he used most of his savings and all the back pay earned in Vietnam. In return for constantly risking his life, a buck sergeant was paid $265 a month, plus an additional $65 combat bonus, all of it tax-free. What a country! Why periwinkle? Who knows, the car salesmen are still laughing.

We soon realized that the car, much less its color, was irrelevant. It was never used except for trips to a liquor store or to check on his crab nets. Pip had decided he was never leaving his room! As the months rolled by, we tried incessantly to reason with him from every angle we could muster. Naturally, he dug in, refused to discuss his latest God-awful decision, and clammed up.

Once again, Pip became a significant pain in the ass. Whenever one of us would drop by, he was always sitting on his bed, surrounded by mounds of crab shells and empty beer cans. He loved watching soap operas on his bedroom TV and soon acquired the ability to follow several story lines simultaneously.

True, none of us had ever been blown up, "much less twice." Still, it was becoming obvious something had to give. Understandably,   Mr. B ran out of patience and placed a padlock on the basement refrigerator protecting his beer.

Pip found his father's actions extremely abrasive because his thirst for adult beverages was growing each month. In addition, until he got a job, he was no longer welcome at family meals. The result was an increased dependency on local waterways for sustenance. People say, "Where there's a will, there's a way." Pip is the most willful guy I've ever met.

He drove back and forth to his secret spot, which was remotely located on a bank of the Hudson River. Fishing was strictly prohibited because the river was heavily polluted. Ignoring all the "warning no fishing" posters, he dropped his crab nets every morning and returned each afternoon. For several months, Pip sat in his bedroom, eating polluted crabs and drinking his father's beer.

Soon, his mother stopped slipping him the refrigerator key. Worse, he was broke, having invested his fortune in the "periwinkle express." Since he had no money for gas, the crabs were safe, but every other living creature, insect, and edible plant within walking distance was doomed. Down to about 130 pounds, it was apparent that hunger was never going to break his will. However, his inability to acquire adult beverages finally compelled him to get off his bed and try living again.

Unfortunately, his resume reflected a woeful absence of previous work experience. Like the rest of us, Pip soon discovered that most employers were opposed to hiring Vietnam Veterans. The media endlessly described us as murderers, baby killers, and drug addicts. In addition, while he was overseas, the protestors, draft dodgers, and deserters had acquired their undergraduate degrees. Most of them now held middle management positions, and having a Vietnam Veteran around was hard on their self-esteem.

Since his service was limited to a mere "conflict," not a war, elected officials shirked their responsibilities and never acted to end the discrimination. Why bother, since most of them and their families had refused to serve? The Veterans of Foreign Wars and the American Legion declined to extend assistance and considered Vietnam veterans to be losers and whiners. Pip learned the hard way; he had to remove any reference indicating military service from his resume. There were also additional contributing factors, not the least of which was his loss of hearing. He could not understand why the job market for hunters and trappers was so limited. After all, he reasoned, "1860 or 1960, people still have to eat!?"

That last pearl of wisdom echoed a new low, even for Pip, and the guys decided it was time for a drunk-a-thon. It was clear that Pip was on the verge of heading out to an area where buses don't run. Out in the area where all the sidewalks are broken and the street lights don't work. Going back to his room was not an option. After the drunk-a-thon got rolling, we started with an easy one by suggesting he might be slightly misinterpreted about what century we lived in.

Nope, not our boy! He went on a rant, restating his position that "people have to eat." As always, he refused to discuss it further and went mute. "So, let it be written, so let it be done," vintage Pip. It took us Friday night, all day Saturday, and Sunday morning to outdrink the bastard. Finally, his mind, along with his will, lost focus. Somewhere between hallucinations and passing out, he relented and mumbled that we might have a minor point, a long shot at best. That was as good as it ever got with him, and we ran with it.

As with all things, a compromise was reached between him and his parents. Pip would enroll in a newly opened local college as a commuter. Also, he would apply for college assistance under the GI bill and work summers for his father. Low tuition combined with financial assistance and summer income would cover his path to an undergraduate degree and future employment. He even promised to respect his dad's property and agreed to a beer ration! So, the lock was quickly removed from the fridge, and just as quickly, Pip broke his promise regarding the beer ration. Well, you can't have everything, "people in hell want ice water."

Maybe there is a God; the periwinkle express bounced back and forth between college and home. Pip was finally happy, racking up passing grades and even joining the on-campus Vietnam veterans' fraternity (They were unwelcome in the other fraternities). Since the frat house had a bar, he mastered improved social skills, which soon paid off. "Hallelujah," Pip even landed a part-time job bartending in a local pub!

During a day of fishing, we asked, "What field of computer science are you specializing in?"

To which he replied, "Computers? I'm not studying computers." The guy was infuriating; he always found a way to drive us crazy. He could drain your patience and deplete your energy faster than a dead battery. Rob and Pip were more than friends; they lived close to each other and grew up enjoying shared experiences. They differed on some things, but never fought about those differences. For example, Rob's religious beliefs followed the accepted norm for 1970. Pip, on the other hand, felt closest to his creator while on a mountain top watching the sun rise. Anyway, the guys decided to let Rob take the lead on this one.

Rob asked, "OK, OK, what are you studying?"

"Biology, Zoology, Anthropology, and Botany, you know all the neat stuff," Pip replied.

Rob asked him, "What are you majoring in?"

"I haven't decided yet," he told him. "Look, Pip, you're in your junior year of college. Is there a guidance counselor or someone on campus helping you study for a degree?" He started to get miffed, but before he could shut down, Rob tried to reason with him.

In a soft tone, Rob explained, "I see why you like those courses so much. They revolve around everything you love: hunting, trapping, and fishing. You're the modern equivalent of a Native American studying to become a medicine man." Damn, Rob made sense; 1860 all over again, he hit the nail on the head. He continued, "But there is an important difference: when the medicine man dies, the new medicine man has an entire tribe to support him, and you don't." You could tell Pip was chewing on that, so Rob continued from another angle, "Suppose you went downstairs, opened the refrigerator, and it was empty? What if there was no one to shop for more beer?" Bingo, Pip met with a guidance counselor and majored in environmental sciences. During his last four semesters, he endured what he referred to as bull—t courses, such as math and English.

One night, he explained to us, "I am not going to spend my life sitting in a box within a box tapping on a hunk of plastic." That was his description of a computer programmer toiling inside an office building cubicle. The guys reasoned that the post-Vietnam Pip was more aware of how fragile life was and determined to enjoy every minute left in his. His attitude seemed plausible for someone closely familiar with high explosives.

Pip managed to graduate and earn his degree. All the guys were proud of his incredible accomplishment, especially considering his humble beginnings, including access to a campus beer hall and a bartending job. I wasn't the only one who lost money in the pool that day. Just what type of job does a modern medicine man, psychologically stuck in 1860, apply for? Simple, he was hired by the state police for a position in their "fish and game" division.

Alone, Pip patrolled deep in the forest each night, stalking poachers and illegal hunters. They also carried firearms, but up against our 1860 mountain man, they never had a chance. He loved it and was good at it, retiring 25 years later as a captain. The state police considered our pain in the ass to be their asset. Through their eyes, jumping from helicopters and patrolling enemy highlands was a positive experience. It is said, "One man's trash is another man's treasure."

Growing up, Pip benefited from Mr. B's know-how and common-sense approach to gardening. Now, coupled with a degree in earth sciences, he morphed into an exceptional gardener. The guy could grow anything in abundance; he made the Jolly Green Giant look like a slug. Once again, his softer side shone through, and local people in need received fresh, healthy produce. The veterans in local VA hospitals ate well because he picked, prepared, and served the food himself.

Sadly, after retiring, Agent Orange entered his life in the form of throat cancer. Part of his recovery included weekly radiation administered on the same side as his good ear (OK 15% of a good ear). The positive long-term result was overcoming throat cancer and the negative was the additional 15% decrease in hearing.

Viable hearing aids were well out of reach for a retiree. Against his better judgment, he decided to investigate whether VA health care was an option. Like his fellow Vietnam veterans, Pip was no exception. For over four decades, he maintained a healthy distance from government. Given a choice, he would never interface with a federal bureaucracy.

I offered to navigate the process with him, and, unaware I was more apprehensive than he was, Pip agreed to the partnership.

Like the only blond on a troop ship, we were naive and vulnerable. The VA pledged to help in any way it could and declared it was solidly behind us. Trust me, we felt them there many times. After completing all the appropriate forms, we sent them "certified mail receipt requested" to the Veterans Affairs Office located in the county seat. Soon, we received confirmation of delivery and waited for a response. We stayed for two months, and none came. Finally, I decided to visit the Veterans Affairs office and inquire as to why we never received a reply.

What I found was a facility staffed by WWII Navy veterans, miffed that I was in their workplace asking pointed questions. At the time, I was unaware of the "hard on" WWII veterans harbored toward Vietnam veterans. My BS detector twitched, so I asked to see the manager and was escorted into his office. The name on the office door matched the name on the registered mail receipt. After the obligatory time spent blowing smoke up each other's ass, I inquired as to the status of our VA health care applications.

He asked, "What applications?" I filled him in on the particulars, gave him copies of the information, and mailed a copy of the "receipt" bearing his name. "I have no idea what happened to these," he said. I suggested he make a few inquiries while I waited. "That won't do any good," he said. "I sent it to the VA hospital, where it was probably lost." At this point, our conversation grew loud, and another rodeo clown entered the room, positioning himself near the door.

"I see," I replied. Give me the name of your contact at the hospital, and I'll drive these copies down to him."

"I can't do that, I don't know who that is," he said.

That response lit my board. I realized I had become a source of amusement for them and just completed lesson one in punching the

VA marshmallow. Since there was nothing left to say or do, I leaned over his desk. Once we were nose to nose, while retrieving my documents, I took the liberty of commenting on his performance as a manager and public servant. "You are as useful as a fart in a spacesuit," I told him and then departed.

Kicking cans, hollering at traffic, and taking deep breaths, I was walking back to my car when I remembered my congressman had an office in the county seat. Before each election cycle, the individual filled my mailbox with endless flyers. On them appeared his broad smiling face and the solemn promise, "My door is always open." So, I headed for his open door. Once off the elevator, the congressional office suite was easy to find. The door to his office was indeed open, and I could see him conversing with political financiers. Unfortunately for me, the office was positioned behind his receptionist and a sea of volunteers.

As advertised, he was smiling at the political hacks strolling through his office door with "plain brown envelopes" in hand. After waiting an hour, a volunteer told me the congressman was just too busy to meet with me, but if I wanted, I could leave a note. Obviously, my congressman wasn't going to give me anything, not even the sweat off his lavalier, much less a meeting. Skunked again, I suggested the volunteer could put Congressman Chuckles and his note where the sun didn't shine and headed back to my car.

Once home, I took pen in hand and composed a detailed letter to the President of the United States. Half a century later, I am still holding my hand on my ass waiting for an answer. What a surprise, "the leader of the free world" was just another pant load politician waxing his tug boat in Washington, DC, collecting a check. When two combat veterans asked for a bit of help, county, state, and federal "public servants" lined up to defecate in our dream boat.

Pip had had enough, preferring to be deaf rather than deaf and reduced to a source of amusement. That sort of attitude gave the VA a chubby; they wanted Vietnam veterans to die and go away. I, on the other hand, decided to push it further. It is said, "Some people are born with a short fuse."

Somewhere between the birth canal and the nursery, someone or something must have angered me. As a result, I have always had a recessed fuse. So, I swallowed my self-respect and asked my son to accompany me to the VA hospital. All those years under the bridge, and I was still apprehensive about setting foot on federal property alone without backup.

I found the eligibility section, spent some time in the waiting room, and eventually wound up in an office. The administrator posed a long string of standard questions along with those stemming from her review of my DD214, military personnel file. Amazingly, after more than four decades, I was able to answer all but one from memory. The lady kept asking, "Where was I in Vietnam and when was I there?"

Each time I answered, "I don't know." When she asked for the fourth time, I ramped up the emphasis and told her, "Look, I wasn't on a vacation tour; the sergeant told us to get on the track, and then we went wherever the hell he told us." Since I didn't know shit about VA procedures, the relevance of the question never registered.

Eventually, "new patient processing" ended, and she pressed enter. When I got up to leave, I was handed a form and told my appointment would be in two weeks. "What appointment?" I asked.

"Your Agent Orange screen," she replied.

"My what?" I asked. She turned to leave, saying,

"When you get to the hospital, they'll explain it to you."

The last time I heard that routine, I was still on active duty, and just like last time, my rear end puckered. I explained, "Lady, I'm just

looking for a little copay on aspirin, I don't want to buy the hospital!"
Just like last time, she was unresponsive and halfway down the hall.

***

Two weeks later, I was lying on a stainless-steel table with a doctor
at each end rattling their findings out loud while Nurse Ratched
entered them into (what else) a computer. I spent the entire day at the
hospital, always at the end of a waiting room line. After they drained
all my precious bodily fluids, I received a chest X-ray and EKG. By
mid-afternoon, they had finally finished, and naturally, I asked about
the results.

I was told to go home, and I would be notified in two weeks.
"How?" I asked.

"Just go to the clinic, they'll explain all of it there."

"What clinic?" I asked.

"You will be contacted by your "primary care provider."

Isn't that peachy keen?" I thought. Skunked again, after four
decades, I was dealing with another government circle jerk.

***

Unfortunately, I soon found out more than I wanted to know about
Agent Orange, Agent Blue, Agent Purple, and the rest of the rain-
bow. They are very toxic herbicides mixed with jet fuel, which is also
harmful to humans. When handled with care, the chemicals pose
no problem, but there was a serious problem. Government wizards
with the IQ of a Martian soil sample ordered daily application of the
chemicals throughout Vietnam. Not one of them gave a fat rat's ass

about the American troops on the ground. No wonder the VA wanted to know "Where I was and when I was there."

Driving home after my day at the beach, I started kicking myself for going against my better judgment. Then I remembered how I became involved in the first place. Thinking about Pip at home drinking cold ones, watching "The Old and the Chest less," resentment began to grow. Come hell or high water, he was going to get a dose of what I just went through. I headed toward his house, pondering how I could convince him to accompany me back to the VA eligibility office.

He was watching TV in his living room, half in the bag; one of his favorite shows, "As the stomach churns," was ending. "Do you like this soap?" he asked.

"No, Pip," I don't watch soaps," I told him.

He persisted, "Why not? They're perfect."

Because I couldn't figure out "Who the hell is screwing who," I countered, before he could continue his sales pitch, I told him that I had successfully enrolled in the VA health care system. Obviously, he was not impressed because he resumed concentrating on his soap, reading the actor's lips. After being bounced two weeks earlier by a government he fought for, his attitude was understandable.

He was done with the VA and was not going to waste time discussing it further, which is exactly what the VA strives for in Vietnam veterans. I resigned myself to the long process of trying to reason with him when I finally hit on a solution. Standing in front of the TV, ensuring good eye contact, I slowly mouthed, "The VA hospital is on Federal property, so you can buy beer tax-free!" "Did I lie?" Yes. "Did he agree to go to the hospital?" Of course. The following week, we passed through a revolving door into the hospital lobby, where an egg sandwich-eating angel of mercy pointed the way toward the eligibility office.

Seated in the waiting room, I asked him, "What's in the large envelope?"

Naturally, I assumed it contained his DD214 and other pertinent documents. Silly me, not our boy, "stuff I found in my sock drawer," he explained. Then he continued, "A p38 can opener, VC flag, local newspaper cuttings about my Purple Hearts, dog tags, photos, and some other stuff." Vintage Pip, after setting up an appointment and driving an hour to the hospital, never considered bringing any written documentation.

I was mouthing the appropriate adjective when he was called into the office. Of course, I rose to go with him, but he pushed me down and put his hand up. In a demeaning tone, he said, "This is a private meeting; you can wait out here."

So, Pip, deaf as a post, entered the office alone.

Through the open office door, I could hear the hospital administrator loudly hollering instructions and questions. The entire hospital, including me, could listen to Pip shouting his responses. I distinctly heard, "How the hell do I know where I was? The chopper hovered, I jumped out, and they returned a couple of days later!"

When asked for documentation, he dumped a large envelope full of memories onto her desk. The expression on the administrator's face, along with the pile of trash on her desk, signaled the meeting was not going smoothly.

Fortunately for Pip, his driver's license, vehicle registration and service serial number helped her find his records. After a five-minute rapid exchange, the lady turned the computer screen towards Pip and, in a booming voice, informed him, "You were never in Vietnam!"

Getting kicked in Alvin and the Chipmunks was one thing, but hearing those words shook Pip down to his soul. With a purple heart in each hand, he began to bellow in disbelief regarding the computer report. Of course, he was "punching the VA marshmallow," and any use of common sense or sound reasoning was useless. Clutching the envelope of memories, he bounced off a wall while exiting her office. Completely crushed, he looked like someone run over by a herd of ravenous elephants. I questioned him about what just happened, but he went dead silent. The truth is that the VA almost sent him back to eating polluted crabs, isolated in his room.

He didn't utter a single word as we made our way back through the hospital, across the parking lot, down the exit road, and along local roadways onto the interstate.

Pip and I were friends for a long time, and I knew if he didn't want to talk, any attempt at conversation was useless. Still, based on what just happened, I became concerned and decided to poke the bear. After all, what are friends for? So, I told him, "Hey Pip, not for nothing, but if you were never in Vietnam, your lying could get me in a lot of trouble." That set him off like a bottle rocket, absolutely "bat shit crazy!" Angry as a sprayed roach, he unleashed a litany of curses laced with spittle in my general direction.

The situation was made worse since I had no beer in the truck, but there was a bright side. Pip was successfully enrolled in the VA health care system. Now it was my turn to remain silent. I was absolutely, positively certain no force in the galaxy could make me accompany Pip for his Agent Orange Screen. All the egg sandwich-eating angels of mercy down at the VA were about to get a good dose of lunatic, and it was Pip's turn to be violated.

Payback is a bitch.

Chapter Ten

GYPSY NIGHTMARE

D *eeply loved by his mother and father, Mickey wanted for noth-ing. His dad was of the Jewish persuasion, and his mother was a Native American. She was serious about her religion having recently converted to Catholicism and doted on him endlessly. Mickey was the only kid I knew with a roll bar on his tricycle. He was eight years old before he found out bread had crust. Smothered by parental love, Mickey never left life's starting line. -Walter*

***

I cannot understand why Mickey chose to hang out with us, even less why his parents let him. Perhaps it was his way of rebelling against a micro-managed childhood and being constantly smothered by his parents. However, let there be no doubt, Mickey was one of the guys fully vested in where life took us. He experienced the "thrill of victory and the agony of defeat" stemming from all our hair-brained schemes.

All that said, "if you looked close enough, you could detect a slight difference in the way he carried himself." Unlike the rest of us, Mickey had a safety net comprised of everything he rebelled against.

One hot summer day, his dad asked him to find out why the cesspool was backing up, an unpleasant job but not very complicated. His dad had already tried the standard solutions, but drain openers and snaking the sewer pipe proved unsuccessful. The task fell to Mickey because his brother no longer lived at home and his father was headed out of town. Mickey, a spoiled brat, was shocked and questioned why his dad didn't call a contractor. The old man explained that their plumber was on vacation. Besides, it was a holiday weekend, which made it impossible to hire a contractor.

Case closed, his dad left town, and the day got hotter, elevating the cesspool stench toward record levels. His initial plan was to do nothing; eventually, his parents would relent and hire a contractor. That approach failed for two reasons: his mother was embarrassed about the stench coming from their backyard, which was becoming abrasive to the neighbors, and his father called repeatedly to check on his progress. For the first time in his life, Mickey was dropped in it up to his neck.

He did what we all did when things got tough and bounced his problem off the guys. After careful deliberation, it became apparent that the guys did not want to touch this one. Mickey panicked, cut to the chase, and offered to pay one hundred dollars for the work. The guys headed home, and I glanced at Larry.

As usual, I was broke, but Larry was worse off and owed money to some of the guys. Larry told him we would take care of the repairs, but we wanted half up front. The meeting broke up, Larry repaid his loans, and we headed toward Mickey's house.

Standing in the backyard, I told Larry, "Well, pal, brutal reality has bitten me once again. Sister Thomas was right, here I am shoveling shit."

Being a true realist, Larry replied, "It may be shit to you, but it's bread and butter to me." Starting at the house, we began to expose the pipe, working our way toward the cesspool. The obstruction was located only two feet from the tank. It was then that Larry looked up to see Mickey smiling down at us, eating a bologna sandwich, sucking on an ice-cold Coke. He was thrilled we solved his problem. The only work left to do was to remove the blockage, repair the open section of pipe, and backfill the trench.

Just then, so close to being finished, the day went south in a hurry. Covered in sweat, sludge, and unknown bodily fluids, I heard Larry ask for lunch! He was the only human being on the face of this earth who would think of bologna and mayonnaise while standing in a shit hole.

Mickey told him, "You'll have to make your own, my mother went out. The kitchen door is open and the bread is on the counter."

Leaning on my shovel, I tried to decide which one of them was the bigger idiot. Moving to sit on the edge of the trench, I watched the debacle play out in slow motion.

Larry, his pants still dripping, shoes encrusted with waste, ambled through the side door into a spotless kitchen. Totally oblivious to the carnage he was causing, he yelled to Mickey, "Where do you keep the mustard?"

I thought, "Well, I know one family eating out this week."

You could hear him whistling as he banged through kitchen cabinets and, with a hint of frustration in his voice, hollered, "Where do you hide the pickles and potato chips?"

What I did not hear was any sound coming from a faucet; it was a good bet Larry had not washed his hands.

Mickey's mom was a very devout woman, as evidenced by her backyard shrine to Mary Magdalen. In remembrance of her deceased mother, she kept a prayer card in the kitchen bread box. Of course, our bologna detective found it and loudly exclaimed, "Holy s—t, I found a God card in the bread box!" He fell into a fit of laughter.

The scream let out by Mickey's mother quickly drowned out all the laughter. Right there in the middle of her kitchen, now resembling a sewerage treatment plant, she saw Larry holding her mother's prayer card in his s—t-covered hands. Mickey tried to calm his mom as she wiped the prayer card, sobbing in disbelief. All the drama cost Larry his appetite, and we headed for the back yard.

After finishing the repairs and filling in the trench, Larry remembered the final payment was due and set out for the kitchen door. When loud knocking went unanswered, he started on the doorbell. Mickey ripped open the door and, waving his arms, told us to go away. Larry stood his ground, "Not so fast, you still owe me $50."

Slamming the door closed, Mickey replied, "You aren't getting jack s—t!"

As we walked home, Larry fumed, "That pant load is going to pay for this!" His anger grew; he began to rant, cursing and waving his arms. Emotionally distraught, he failed to notice people gagging as they passed by us. It's a safe bet his poor unsuspecting Mother gagged when she went to do his laundry. Larry may have been a "D" student, but when ill-treated, he never forgot or forgave; there was no doubt Mickey would pay for stiffing him. By the way, the grass is always greener on top of the septic tank.

Naturally, the town's swimming pool complex included a men's changing room. Instead of a door, you entered through a wide

L-shaped cinder block passageway. It was a sparse room equipped with nothing but a few benches. As a result, everyone changed in full view of the other swimmers.

During one lazy day in August, Larry whispered he had an idea how to break the monotony. Arguably, Mickey was the best-looking member of the gang and well-funded. He dated several young ladies and was known by all. Now God has a sense of humor, and it just so happened that "our Jewish Indian" was the only one of us not circumcised!? Late that afternoon, we put Larry's scheme into action.

Pip was assigned the task of mingling with the bon-bon beauties to warn them that we had found a giant poisonous snake in the men's changing room.

They listened intently as he explained, "Only Mickey was brave enough to catch the dastardly viper." Sure, he had their attention, he went on, "If you want to see the massive serpent walk over by the men's locker room."

Meanwhile, the rest of us sat on benches waiting patiently for Mickey to drop his bathing suit. Within minutes, we had him stripped "balls ass naked" and after a brief scuffle, threw him out of the locker room. He regained his balance and began cursing at us, then he heard loud shrieks of laughter. Turning around, he was mortified when he realized he had landed in front of the snack bar.

Immediately, just as Larry promised, we heard loud squeals along with OH's and Ah's. All the bob bon beauties covered their eyes while the painted Trollips with fingers spread wide did the same. What we learned to our surprise was that young ladies frequently discuss and compare lavaliers! Who knew? Based on their expert summation, Mickey, circumcised or not, was deemed to be "hung like a bull mouse."

Apparently, "Alvin and the Chipmunks" were unimpressive, and he scored low. The only positive was abundant curiosity in his unusual, misshapen member. As a result, his social life boomed, and it became commonplace to find notes scotch-taped to his locker. Mickey never thanked us, but we were quick to forgive his lapse in good manners. After all, what are friends for?

It became apparent that any port (ok, lavalier) in a storm would do on a Saturday night. Each note read like a short resume, complete with name, phone number, and suggested activities such as a movie, dance, or party. Eye and hair color were optional. Naturally, the nuns disapproved and tore up everything taped to his locker; we suspected they read them first, but couldn't prove it.

Mickey was the younger of two boys. His older brother suffered from epilepsy and gave little warning prior to experiencing a fit. One evening at our watering hole in upstate New York, Mickey consumed too much and got into a pushing match with the local bed bugs. Since he suffered from mental irregularity, he failed to recognize how many locals he was up against or that they were about to kick his ass.

He was one of us, which left no option other than being sucked into the mayhem. I don't remember much, but the bartender was kneeling on the bar, swinging a baseball bat. He was trying to hit Mickey as he ran round and round the bar chasing some hick with his butter knife. Then, one country bumpkin hurled a shot glass, hitting me just above the temple. I dropped like a stone, good night nurse, just inside the front door.

I woke up in the county hospital, looking at a state trooper who asked, "Why did you start the fight?" Looking down, I could see my bloody shirt and pants. Telling him I wasn't there or didn't know what he was talking about would be fruitless. Then I remembered, I went down just inside the front door, so I played the only card I had. I explained, "Officer, I opened the door, was knocked out, and woke up here. Honestly, I don't know anything."

He looked at me and grunted, "Honest, huh?" He continued, "Then why did the other guys tell me you started the fight?"

Just then, my incredible headache took second place to the anger building in me. I asked him, "Would you please have my pals step in here?"

"Nope, they're all down in the county jail," he informed me. Either he did not have enough to pin the debacle on me, or he felt sorry for the bloody mess in front of him. Either way, he let me go and, based on my condition, extended the courtesy of giving me a ride down to the county lock-up.

As we pulled up, it was evident that everyone had made bail. Gathered on the front lawn, they resembled the fight scene in a Mexican western. In one corner, Pip, with his head down, was getting a loud talk from his dad. Rob was quietly listening to his shocked, animated father, and Larry was trying to protect himself from his mom's kicks and punches. Luke and Dip, still drunk, were vomiting on a parked police car. Apparently, the other parents bailed them out.

Mickey was punching it out with his brother right on the police department's front lawn! His sobbing Mom was praying her rosary while watching her sons beat the hell out of each other. Just before round two, Mickey's brother suffered a fit. Looking through his windshield at the Olympian display of insanity, the trooper asked, "Do you really hang out with these assholes!?"

The following week, during our card game, it occurred to me that I was the only one of us not facing out-of-state charges. All of them would soon be in court, looking at a string of charges from assault to property damage. Of course, I was still pissed off that they informed the police that I started the riot, and less than thrilled about them leaving me in a doorway to die.

So, I decided to poke the bear and told them, "Don't worry, I'll come to visit you buffoons in the big house. Maybe I'll bake a cake with a file in it." The guys chewed on that for a few minutes. Then the bastards had the balls to ask me for a "thank you," adding, "Hey, what are friends for!?"

About a month later, Mickey called and asked me to stop by. The request was nothing special; the guys would visit each other and, on occasion, hang out for the entire day. But not this time, this time it was different. There was no way I could have known Larry and Mickey had spent the week working on Larry's latest money-making "wet dream.".

Mickey opened the door, dressed like a gypsy nightmare. His hair was done up in a jelly roll, complete with duck tails. He was wearing a red beret, a silk pink shirt two sizes too large, black pants two sizes too small, black silk sox, pointy shoes, and a wide gold chain complete with a four-inch-long crucifix.

Taken by surprise, I asked, "Did you get a bowl of soup with that shirt? Did those shoes come off a witch?" I became frightened when Larry walked up behind him wearing the same clown suit! Once inside, I asked, Ehh...Ahh...Hi guys, "I give up. What's going on? Halloween is still a few months away, right?"

Larry became so excited that he was bouncy as he blathered, "Do you like it? All the guys in the "Del Royals" will wear stuff like this!" My mind warned my mouth, "No, no, no, shut up and leave. You've been down this road before."

Mickey slipped in between me and the door as he explained, "We're starting a band and we want you to play drums. Larry is playing rhythm guitar, and I play lead guitar. I know this guy, Mike, who plays sax, and Tony agreed to be our lead singer. Tony has a station wagon, only one kidney, and a nasal blockage!"

I asked him, "Who is Mike? What the hell is a Del Royal? How can a kidney cause nasal blockage?"

Once again, Larry figured out a way to make easy money. He was on a roll, and nothing was going to stop him. True, after years of lessons, I could play the drums, and each of them played a decent guitar. Still going on stage and performing at a large high school dance was a whole different thing. Experience taught me logic and common sense were useless once Larry smelled money, much less adoring female fans. I was doomed.

During the next two weeks of band practice, I learned: On stage, a "Del Royal" also wore a rented purple and black Maharaja jacket (Jesus!), due to his nasal blockage, Tony's voice was "to be kind" unique, and Mike knew how to play a sax.

In addition, I found out Harry booked us for a sweet sixteen party at $100. The local magistrate planned the surprise party for his daughter and actually paid for a plywood stage in his backyard.

A week later, on a beautiful summer evening, I was back at the house getting into my Del Royal costume.

I glanced at Mickey, surprised to see him stuff a pair of rolled-up socks into the fly of his pants. Mickey, I said, "You do know we're playing at a Judge's house?"

"Yeah, so?" he replied while adjusting his roll of socks, and I don't mean the silk ones over his pointy shoes.

I thought, "Mental note, never again will I drive a car through that magistrate's town."

Things went smoothly, we were a hit, and I relaxed. A bit too soon because our "star lead guitarist" began to jump up and down, causing him to fall through the plywood stage. Still clutching his electric guitar, he produced amplified squealing all the way down. The shrieking from Mickey startled the crowd and, coupled with our uncontrolled laughter, was enough to get the Judge's attention. He jogged into his backyard, surprised to see Mickey's feet sticking up through his broken stage. It was then I thought, "Maybe the State Trooper was right, I should find new people to hang out with."

Turned out the Judge was a good guy. His only concern was for Mickey, and he joined in to help us free our "rock star" from the mangled stage.

The stage had collapsed inward, pinning Mickey along with his guitar and amp below shards of wooden framing and plywood. Freeing him from the rubble that he created required some tools and considerable effort.

The anger stemming from embarrassment and his endless bitching and moaning were not helpful, but we freed him without injury.

From then on, the painted trollips considered him to be more of a comedian than a rock star. We made sure everyone knew his mother dressed him before the party, socks and all. Hey, what are friends for?

Then the judge saw Mike's sax lying on the stage where he had dropped it, and the condoms previously hidden inside were lying on the stage.

Case closed; court adjourned! He quickly ruled that his daughter's sweet sixteen party was over, and I beat a path toward the station wagon.

Looking around, I asked Tony, "Where's Larry?"

Tony replied, "He went back to get paid for tonight!" Naturally, no one was paid, and I never drove through that town again.

The last kick in my Tallywacker was when Mickey told me, "You owe $35 for the jacket rental!"

What do you do with a new band coming off a terrible first performance? If you're Larry, you find a large regional high school and book the senior dance. The consummate optimist, Larry's glass was always half full, usually with rum and Coke. God must have a sense of humor because the Del Royals became a hit, and soon local high schools requested us.

The five band members were paid $100 per performance, but the rental cost for each Maharaja jacket was $35. Arithmetic was never Larry's best subject; you do the math.

During the 1960s, diners greatly outnumbered fast food restaurants. After 11:00 p.m. on a weekend night, the diner was your only option. Since most dances ended at 11:00, we usually ate around 1:00 a.m. before going home and became very familiar with the menu at each eatery. It made no difference which establishment we ate at because the standard order for everyone, except Dip, was a cheeseburger, fries, and a Coke. Dessert was always apple pie with vanilla ice cream.

Not Dip, he insisted on ruining every meal by ordering "liver and bacon," which he washed down with unsweetened iced tea. His favorite dessert was rice pudding "with raisins" no less.

Mickey found the smell and appearance of liver so offensive that he lost weight on weekends. Finally, he broke down, swearing, "I can't watch Dip eat road kill again. I'll drive tonight; I found a dinner that doesn't sell that God awful stuff." So, we piled into his mother's pristine Ford sedan and set out for Mickey's "no liver" diner. Sedans in the late 1960s came standard with bench seats front and back. Even with two bench seats after the seven of us squeezed in it looked like a clown car.

His route took us into the city on a congested three-lane highway. Apparently, Jewish Indians prefer driving in the center lane; as a result, we sped forward at 50 MPH surrounded by tractor-trailers. A truck rode our bumper with another in front, while others whizzed by on each side. It is evident that driving fast in heavy congestion was making Mickey nervous, but he began to get accustomed to it.

Everyone settled in, looking forward to a good meal with friends on a pleasant summer night. About then, Dip yelled, "I dropped my cigarette lighter behind the seat and can't find it!"

Luke told him, "Relax, run your hand along the seam and feel for it."

"It was lit when I dropped it, you feel for it!" Dip replied.

Rob joined in, "I see smoke, the seats are on fire!"

Mickey was listening to the chaos unraveling in the back of his car. Tightly boxed in by tractor-trailers traveling at high speeds, listening was about all he could do.

The back of his car filled with smoke, and Rob squealed, "We have to do something, there's a gas tank back here!"

With the rear windows open wide, Mickey's car emitted a smoke trail reminiscent of a damaged WWII fighter plane plummeting toward earth. Glancing at our "pilot," I watched him turn white and start shaking like a crack baby on a jackhammer; he was clutching the steering wheel in a death grip. Just when I thought things couldn't get any worse, they did. Luke yelled, "Quick, pull the seat bottom up, then forward. I'll open the door."

The overhead dome light came on, and Mickey went rigid as his mother's smoking rear seat was launched high into a truck lane. Within seconds, a sixteen-wheeler discovered it, and the resultant squealing, splintering, and crushing sound caused Mickey to flinch.

After the seat's brutal death, everything fell silent; the only sound was Dip negotiating more room on the car floor. The silence was quickly shattered when Mickey snapped and went crazy as an outhouse rat! His rant started with, "Jesus, Mary, and Joseph!"

Rob, drawing on strong religious beliefs, cut him short, "Hey, they had nothing to do with it!" Now, Rob may have had good intentions, but his timing was atrocious.

As a result, Mickey began blaspheming everyone ever mentioned in the bible, both the Old and New Testaments.

He was still on a roll when we pulled into the diners' parking lot. Tired of all the drooling academy drama, the guys strolled into the choke and puke looking for a window table. His voice lowered, Mickey still wouldn't let go, "What do I tell my mother? She's going to be so disappointed in me."

We told him, "We understand, especially since you're a constant source of disappointment to us."

That lit his board, but before he could start another rant, Luke explained, "Listen, you should be thanking us; we saved you from dying in a flaming crash." After all, "What are friends for?"

Luke's admonishment sent Mickey apoplectic, and he lost the ability to speak. Based on his contorted face, he appeared to be having a stroke or some other kind of seizure. Either way, it didn't matter, since it gave us a chance to focus on the best way to BS his mother and father. He was given two options: his parents should be grateful he survived Ford's horrendous back-seat assembly plant procedures, or he could lament on the new trend in car theft that specialized in stealing parts only, such as rear seats.

Problem solved, we finally settled down to order dinner. As we scanned our menus looking for specialty burgers, Mickey let out a loud groan. He stared in disbelief at the new daily special, "liver with onions." Totally drained, he sat motionless as the waitress placed our burgers, along with Dip's liver and onions, on the table. Taking pity on him, Dip offered to change his order. Instead of rice pudding with raisins, just this one time, he ordered cherry pie with whipped cream. Hey, what are friends for?

Chapter Eleven

TROUBLED GIANT

L uke *lived his life constantly balancing optimism, pessimism, and realism. Deep in thought, he carefully listened to and observed people before speaking. Stroking his beard and always smoking a Lucky Strike, he appeared old and wise for his age. A natural problem solver, Luke's sage advice was appreciated at many a "Drunk-A-Thon." However, like all things, there was a downside. Luke was a troubled soul, and his emotions ran deep. It was easy to tell when there were problems at home because he said less and smoked more.*

– Walter

***

Like a moth to a flame, Luke's attraction to our little gang of misfits was inevitable; most of us functioned devoid of family, and Luke was no exception. We learned to rely heavily on one another for the strength and wisdom typically provided by biological parents and/or siblings. Over time, our friendships morphed into a surrogate family. Better than love, we respected each other and appreciated spending time together. Unorthodox as it may have seemed, the result was a strong nucleus from which each of us drew emotional and financial stability. Life was easier with guaranteed unconditional support just a phone call away.

Typical of deep thinkers, Luke was far from the life of the party. He was not anti-social, but small talk was not his forte, and he rarely initiated a conversation.

On occasion, a friend from his football team would meet him in our upstate bar. I watched them sit next to each other in complete silence for up to ten minutes at a time. Luke downing candle glows while his friend, suffering from ulcers, nursed his white Cadillac. Giggle if you must, and snicker if you will. Luke considered that to be a "good time.

Mickey would fall deeply in love with any girl who so much as looked at him. Each heart throb zoomed from acquaintance to fiancée in just a few weeks.

Not Luke, he was the direct opposite. There was one and only one sweet young thing for him. Attracted to her in grammar school, he dated her throughout high school and college. They married and to this very day continue to enjoy life together. Some outside our "family" considered Luke's preference concerning "matters of the heart" as odd. To better understand his mindset, they only had to take a closer look at his earlier years.

Like the rest of us, Luke had his strengths and weaknesses. Always dependable, he never dodged responsibilities, traits that Larry and Dip exploited. Compared to the rest of us, they were small in stature, but that never stopped them from causing endless problems. It's always a sure bet that some little guy started the bar fight. No matter what the venue, ballpark, race track, beach, or bar, they could start shit faster than spicy chili in a retirement home. Before exchanging insults could become exchanging punches, the guys would gather to show their support. Luke, Walter, and Mickey were of ample size, and the seven of us presented a unified front. If Lady Luck smiled and the fight was averted, the only thing left to do was muzzle Larry and Dip.

Large when compared to other high school students, Luke weighed in at well over two hundred pounds, and being six feet tall, he was a big boy. Lifting endless cases of books only added to his intimidating appearance. We knew he was a troubled yet gentle soul, but no one else did. Vince Lombardi, a sports legend, coached Luke's high school varsity football team. When he spotted Luke in the freshman class, he had an orgasm. By junior year, Luke was starting at left tackle on a state championship team.

The end result was a "troubled giant" trained and conditioned to unleash short bursts of violence. Those attributes, when added to his dark side, induced society to classify him as a reject. In contrast, our eclectic family was blessed with one more brother from another mother. We stayed close to Luke, suspecting serious jail time was only one trigger away.

It was a very different time, long before DYFS and women's rights. Abuse stemming from a drunken father or husband was considered an embarrassment and never discussed outside the home. Luke's old man, often inebriated, found time on weekends to remind Luke and his mother about their shortcomings and, on occasion, preach about the financial burden they wreaked upon him. Unfortunately, Luke's alcoholic Father was not a sports fan and was totally unaware of Luke's physical transformation.

One weekend, Luke got away from us. To protect his mother and himself, he warned Dad they were no longer going to debate family affairs until he sobered up. Offended, the old man threw a misplaced right cross, and in return, Luke cold cocked him in the living room. When he regained consciousness, due to alcohol and/or a concussion, he made a serious error in judgment and told Luke to get out of his house. His actions were miscalculated at best because they left Luke with nothing to lose. Before departing, just for shits and giggles, he placed a few more punches in the old man's beer gut. That dropped him into his recliner, where he sat quietly while Luke gave him a dose of brutal reality, "You touch mom again and I'll shove your gonads down your throat and rip your heart out."

After their father and son chat, Luke kissed his mom and left home. His next move was to call the guys, and that night, an emergency "Drunk-A-Thon" was held in Pip's basement. Due to short notice, the card game started late, and we braced for an all-nighter. Luke sounded tired as he explained his quality time spent at home. In keeping with established norms, we took turns kicking him while he was down. He was treated to a plethora of: Are you stupid? What the hell is wrong with you? You're an immense pain in my ass. Since he left me on a barroom floor, I piled on, "You haven't got the brains of a flea!" Luke knew berating him was our way of expressing affection. Since none of us were familiar with proper social etiquette, we developed our own norms of behavior.

Listening to the banter, Rob spoke first, "His dad could go to the cops, and with a swollen mouth, they'll believe him."

After a short pause, Pip gave us more reason for concern, adding, "Don't Luke live in the same town where you buffoons pissed off a judge?"

"Yeah," said Larry. "He's still mad. If Luke gets arrested, that guy will put him so far behind bars, we'll have to feed him with a sling shot." Just like that, our problem became a debacle, good night nurse!

As the night wore on, we broke our big problem down into smaller ones. Luke could sleep in his car, but street parking was not allowed between 1:00 a.m. and 5:00 a.m. Easy solution, Luke could park in my driveway. Meals were served at the corner diner. Bathrooms were available, one at work and another in the diner. Each concern was laid to rest, and we headed home, except for Luke, who no longer had a home.

With both cars tucked in my driveway, I started to say good night, but Luke interrupted. "This isn't going to work," he said. Before I could ask why he continued, "I left my mother holding the bag for what I did. She's home alone with the old man, and that worries me. When he leaves for work tomorrow morning, I want to see her. Actually, I need to check on her every morning, and I can't do that unless I'm close to the house."

Hearing him, I thought, "This guy is emotionally drained. Do I cut him some slack or give him a dose?"

Over the years, I learned the hard way that when dealing with significant problems, you had to function. Looking at a problem through rose colored glasses never accomplishes a thing. Screw it, Luke and the guys never cut me any slack; it was time for a dose. With good eye contact, I told him, "That ship has already sailed and you no longer have a home. Even before you bounced the old man, your mother was facing a rough stretch in her marriage. Maybe you should leave it alone, at least for a few days."

Chewing on my comments, Luke took a seat on his car bumper, and I watched as reality slowly set in. Reality leaves no room to rationalize or compartmentalize, as a result, all the unicorns and rainbows left his head.

The next day, I went to join him for breakfast, but the car was gone. I caught up with him at work and started asking the logical questions.

Luke gave me the "talk to my hand" routine, saying, "I don't want to talk about it." Blindsided and running on three hours of sleep, I unloaded, "Well, that's just peachy, you sure as hell weren't this calm and collective at the drunk-a-thon last night. When the shit hit the fan, you couldn't wait to drop a dime on us, but now you want to play Bobby bad ass? Next time your tits are in a wringer, you can sniff my shorts!"

Luke apologized, and during the conversation, it became apparent we had miscalculated the bond between a mother and son. He went on to explain that while driving around, he found a mill complex down by the river.

After listening to him, we assumed Luke found a garden apartment near his mother with a river view, no less. We were so happy to hear the problem was solved, we forgot who we were dealing with.

Naturally, all of us were anxious to see his new digs, but he refused to invite us over. After a few days, he looked and smelled like a bum that fell off the south end of a northbound freight, and like it or not, we followed him home. One look and we knew he blew smoke up our ass. According to the "Historical Society Plaque" mounted on a pedestal, Luke's "garden apartment" was described as a grist mill built around 1760.

The plaque went on to explain that George Washington slept there. Luke had furnished it in "homeless tramp" complete with a radio, an air mattress, blankets, bottled water, abundant Devil Dogs, Twinkies, and a bucket with two boards across it. The nearby river completed the bathroom décor, explaining his appearance.

This was breathtaking stupidity, a new low, and it shocked us. Mickey was the first to find his voice, "Jesus Luke!"

To which Rob replied, "Jesus had nothing to do with it."

We all replied in unison, "Shut up, Rob," Dam, Luke, what the hell is wrong with you?"

Indignant, he told us, "What? If it's good enough for George Washington, it's good enough for me!" Utilizing the diner sink and a few personal hygiene products, Luke lived in that mill for two weeks.

Thankfully, his aunt came down from Connecticut and took him back with her, enrolling him in the local college. I have no idea which law enforcement department is responsible for protecting our national monuments, but evidently, it takes summers off. Maybe there is a God. Should you have any doubt, ask our apostle, Rob, who prayed for Luke a lot that summer.

Chapter Twelve

STOLEN BRASSIERE

When God passed out brains, Dip thought he said trains and asked for a small one that ran in circles to put under his Christmas tree. He was a piece of work capable of extraordinary genius and unexcelled stupidity. Coupled with a big pair of b---s, Dip never ceased to fascinate. Barely squeaking through, he considered high school to be a waste of time and never gave college a thought. Small in stature, never intimidated by anyone or anything, he harbored gigantic dreams. Come hell or high water, Dip was going to be a success in life, and anyone foolish enough to get in his way would get their a—kicked. Many years later, I had a chance to dine with him and his current bride. I watched as they arrived in "matching high-end luxury cars" and thought, "Never bet against this guy." - Walter

***

During our high school years, Dip amused himself by exasperating the faculty. Since Catholic schools could expel students at any time for any reason without legal ramifications, fellow students considered his behavior either courageous or foolish. They reasoned that eventually he'd get caught in the act and expelled, but they didn't know Dip like we did. Courage and luck had nothing to do with his long-running string of pranks. Dip didn't care if school kept or not, much less getting caught. His life was goal-driven, and he lived at 100 miles an hour; expulsion would be nothing more than a speed bump.

Walking into biology class, if the frogs used for dissection were on the teacher's desk, mounted in a reproductive pose, we knew Dip was in that class. Before the French teacher arrived in his classroom, the students enjoyed all the filthy limericks scribbled on his blackboard. They were written in perfect French, something the guys found confusing since Dip was failing French. Gym class was always fun when "someone" shuffled all the jock straps between the lockers. As a result, during basketball games, Alvin and the Chipmunks either went free range or wound up stuffed in a sardine can. Either way, gym class seldom ended pain-free for anyone except Dip.

High school settled into a rhythm until one day his classmates challenged Dip to pull off the apex of gold standard pranks. Based on the difficulty and danger involved, they sweetened the pot by offering a monetary reward to anyone who could pull it off. The instant they mentioned a monetary reward, Dip's ears stopped listening, and his mind began plotting.

To understand the magnitude, you must consider the point in history (1960) and the surroundings (A large co-ed catholic high school located at a busy intersection). The winning contestant would have to acquire one of the girls' gym suits (her bloomers) and hoist it to the top of a flagpole. Adding to the degree of difficulty, the flagpole was mounted on a pergola three stories above the high school's main entrance.

In addition, the prank had to be completed in absolute secrecy. Should the perpetrator become exposed, the monetary reward would be invalid. It was enough to make Evil Knievel pause, and at the next Drunk-A-Thon, we counseled Dip to forget it. Naturally, our warning was ignored because Dip was drawn to money like a rat to cheese.

***

Ten days later, the Prince Apple, Sister Kevin stood in front of her high school looking up at a pair of bloomers fluttering high in the sky just under the American flag. Hoping for a bonus, Dip added a brassiere stolen from a "well-endowed" gymnast.

Seething, she listened as motorists stopping at the intersection burst into laughter. A woman of the cloth, she could not release her anger in the street, but within the privacy of her office, the poor nun made the devil blush. A janitor was rushed onto the roof with orders to lower the flag, bloomers, and brassiere before someone took a picture.

Always a prime suspect, we listened as the intercom summoned Dip to the Prince Apple's office.

Livid, the school administration accused him of sinful, unforgivable behavior. Dip adamantly denied any involvement and informed them he witnessed students from their religion class crouching and giggling on the roof. They had no proof, and Dip knew it. After collecting his hard-won windfall, he treated us all to dinner at the local "hold your pickle, grab my weenie." Some would argue the guy had no brains, but everyone agreed he had more balls than a billiard table.

It was a point in time when young ladies, on a date, paid for absolutely nothing. All a bob-bon beauty ever wanted to do was have fun, and every one of them could stampede through your wallet faster than a raped buffalo.

On a weekend, if you had no money, the only embrace you enjoyed was with celibacy. In self-defense, the guys used a ranking system to estimate what a date would cost. Low to high rankings ran; oogly, ugly, lovely, pretty, and knock down gorgeous. Expensive enough to begin with, the gorgeous ones came with an additional complication called the double date. They usually had an oogly or ugly best friend, and unless you got her a date too, you could hold your hand on your ass. Since none of the guys would invest in an oogly girl you wound up paying for everyone.

Tapped out for most of the summer, I was seriously considering if "eu-nuch" would be a good career choice and became increasingly aware of Dip's success with the Ladies.

A full-time job wasn't funding his lifestyle because he spent all day hanging out with us. So, I asked him, "How can you afford to date every week?"

"Oh," he said. I have a part-time job."

I asked, "Based on the size of your harem, you must be well paid?"

He answered, "Nah, I get minimum wage working just a few hours each morning, I count garbage trucks down at the dump."

Then I said, "I don't get it. How can you afford prize trollips on minimum wage?"

He explained, "The state charges garbage haulers a fee every time they unload at the landfill. My job is to park at the front gate and keep a handwritten tally of how many loads are dropped by each hauler.

I've met with all of them to discuss my poor memory because I figured out that the serious money is not in counting garbage trucks, it's in "not counting" some of the trucks. Whenever I drop my pencil, somebody's truck enters the dump, and I get a percentage of the savings. The prettier the girl, the more often I lose count." Remember, Walter, there's always money to be made in sewerage and garbage. It may be garbage to you, but it's bread and butter to a politician." Dip never studied earth science in college, but he sure as hell graduated "Summa Cum Laude" in brutal reality.

After thinking a moment, he asked, "The dump is a one-man job, but I also have another job. Do you want in?"

"Hell yes," I said.

The following morning, he drove us to "Rinaldo's Swimming Pools Inc.," located out on the highway. As he pulled into an "employees only" parking spot, I asked, "Are we going to build swimming pools?"

"Not exactly," He replied.

"So, I guess we're going to sell pools," I said.

"Not exactly," He replied. "Stay in the car, I'll be right back." He returned with a handful of folders and headed up the highway, explaining my new career as we drove.

I spoke to the boss and explained, "You, like me, are just barely 17. As a result, you're too young to prosecute as an adult. Congratulations, you now work for Rinaldo's. Our job is to get building permits for above-ground pools, and each folder contains drawings and specifications for a pool already sold. It's not going to be easy to get permits because most towns know about Rinaldo's lousy construction and questionable business practices."

"What do you mean, lousy construction?" I asked.

He went on to explain, "They have a habit of deviating from the approved drawing and specification. For example, the redwood framing was wood from other construction sites; they simply wipe the pine clean and treat it with redwood stain. Also, the specification calls for "portable pools" assembled with stainless steel screws, but it's cheaper and faster to use common nails. Hell, there were even a couple of pools they forgot to put drains in. All of that is nickel-dime because the company declares bankruptcy and changes its name every two years or so."

He continued, "You know minor oversights are common in the construction trade. Anyone can make a mistake or two on the job."

I thought to myself, "Damn, and I thought I was street-wise. This guy makes me look like a babe in the woods. Maybe I should rethink this one."

What Dip said next got my full attention: "Walter, we can work two town halls at the same time. I'll drop you off at one, then stop by another and pick you up on my way back. Since we get $25 cash for each permit, we'll have enough money in just three days to cover four days at the beach. Just imagine how our pockets will jingle? Money attracts pretty girls and pretty girls like to advertise; their bikinis are so small they look like fanny flossers!"

Then I thought, rethink my ass and told him, "Drive faster and teach me how you sell a pool permit."

Dip pulled into our first stop and told me to follow him into the town hall. Before exiting the car, he counted out six fifty-dollar bills and grabbed the folder.

Once inside, he asked to meet with the building inspector, and we watched his face frown when he saw us. "What do you want? He asked. "Need a permit for a Rinaldo above-ground portable pool." Dip responded as he sat down at the guy's desk.

The building inspector sat down across from him and said, "No way, not in this town." Dip told him, "I can think of fifty ways, all of them green."

The inspector replied, "Nope," then paused.

Then Dip told him, "There must be a hundred reasons, all of them green, why this pool should be built."

Again, he said, "Nope." At two hundred reasons, the inspector told us he had to use the men's room and exited the office.

Dip placed four fifty-dollar bills into the job folder. Then he opened the desk drawer, putting the envelope inside, being careful to leave the drawer open a few inches.

Upon his return the inspector removed a permit from the same drawer and signed it. After thanking him we left permit in hand and headed back to the car.

That scenario was repeated all summer long with mixed results ranging from a complete refusal to a three-hundred-dollar donation. When a permit was denied, Dip called Rinaldo, making them aware of the problem. We were never allowed to exceed a three-hundred-dollar donation, and all donations made to "little league teams" by Rinaldo Pools Inc. were carefully logged.

At the end of each day, Dip turned in his log along with any unused "little league" donations. Incomplete job folders went into a bin marked "for further action," and then Dip was paid twenty-five dollars cash for each approved permit.

***

A few days later, I was enjoying all the eye candy sunning in the pool. Sipping an adult beverage, I smiled, thinking about the long list of characters in my life. They taught me many "things not known to kings" along with some essential life lessons. Always respect the religious persuasion of others; you can find saints and devils in any faith. Do not assess anyone based solely upon their chosen lifestyle; we are a product of our surroundings, and the variations in life are endless. Camels do not socialize with fish. It is not wise to prejudge anyone's intelligence based solely on formal education. Stranded in the jungle without a laptop, the computer geek is fair game. In contrast, the primitive hunter could excel with a modern firearm.

Chapter Thirteen

JUNKYARD BOYS

A s time passed, we each obtained a driver's license and looked forward to enjoying the independence that came from owning a car. Larry, Mickey, Pip, and Dip were lucky because their mother or father provided them with their first set of wheels. Rob, Luke, and I were less fortunate. Our situation was abysmal; we were dealing with a long-standing, overwhelming shortage of discretionary income. Our only option was a trip to the local junkyard, where the proprietor was always ecstatic to see us. Sprinkled across his lot were some absolute wrecks. Many of them were total heaps, so unsafe that they were refused entry into the local demolition derby. - Walter

***

He was an absolute sperm ball and referred to his trash on wheels as "mechanical marvels," sharing lineage with only the finest luxury cars. His sales approach included gems like "This one is hardly broken in. You can't buy them like this anymore. Running boards and a rumble seat, luxury you can't find in today's market, and my personal favorite, why would anyone want a tinted windshield? You might as well drive blind folded!" His only terms of sale were cash on the barrel head. Each time he robbed one of us, we stood by dejected while he gleefully skipped into the local pub, his pockets jingling with our golden crinkles.

Mickey never experienced the junkyard. Once he got his license, dear mom "gave him" her car. It was a three-year-old baby blue Ford that she only drove back and forth to church. The mileage was so low when you looked at the odometer; instead of numbers, it read "brand new." Normally, we would have been happy for Mickey and wished him luck with his new wheels.

Inexplicably, Mickey stepped out of character and disparaged us regarding our pathetic choices in private transportation. After calling Rob's Plymouth a "shit box with wheels," He turned to me and said, "The debacle you're driving resembles a junk truck without the truck." I found his ridicule to be abrasive, mainly because it was true.

Pip was fortunate that his parents purchased a used Ford Falcon with the understanding that it would be shared between him and his sister. Who knows what they were thinking? Pip "shared" the car the same way he "shared" his father's beer. Out of gas and parked in the driveway was the only time his sister ever saw it. The upside was a free vehicle in good running condition, but there were a few drawbacks. Ford's Falcon was one of the first subcompacts built by an American car manufacturer. The car was so small it resembled a pregnant roller skate.

One sales feature was very low gas consumption. To understand why it was so fuel-efficient, all you had to do was open the hood. Instead of buying gas, Pip fed lettuce to the dozen gerbils inside running on a treadmill. The car posed no problem for Pip's sister, and all her girlfriends thought it was cute. Pip, on the other hand, endured getting his gonads broken on a regular basis. The guys constantly hung stuff onto his car or placed "gifts" inside of it. He found things like bicycle handlebar grips, playing cards to place in the spokes, small fender reflectors, and the like. Following the established norm, when one of us was down, everyone else piled on, and the wisecracks became endless. Still, you can't have everything; people in hell want ice water. Brutal reality rule #1: Life's not fair.

Larry and his absent father must have discussed his transportation needs. Larry must have laid it on thick because the old man brought him a six-year-old Pontiac in excellent condition. It ran like new; the only downside was the paint job. Pontiac made large cars, and this was black with "caution road construction" bright yellow trim. It looked like a deranged bumblebee on steroids. Still in the jungle cruiser beauty contest, Larry's car would tie for second along with Mickey's. No one was ever going to beat Dip's cadaver chariot.

***

Within one year Larry turned that car into a broken-down junk heap. Its transformation was a direct result of Larry's complete indifference toward even the most basic maintenance requirements. Oil level, transmission fluid, grease, anti-freeze, battery checks and even tire rotation were never addressed. Brakes? Who needs brakes? Sad as Larry's mechanical skills were his inability to pay for even simple repairs made the situation worse. He stormed through a pay check faster than crap through a goose. If air wasn't free, he would have driven around on four flat tires.

In essence the car was a victim of Larry's full blown "four- alarm" life style. When the bar closed, it was always the last car out of the lot.

The closest it ever got to a car wash was when it rained at the drive-in. Its back seat and suspension system strained to keep up with the ebb and flow of Larry's precious bodily fluids. If inanimate objects could commit suicide, that Pontiac would have propelled itself off a cliff in a nanosecond.

When it came to first cars, Dip hit a home run. The guys were parked side by side in a lot down by the river, looking like a hillbilly re-union, when he unexpectedly pulled up in a brand-new Buick station wagon!? Gleaming black, long as a cruise ship, it was luxurious, and I almost pinched a loaf in my jeans. We were immediately on him like white on rice, demanding to know where he got it. He explained, "My uncles own Salabono's funeral home. They heard I got my license and offered me a job. I pick up stiffs when they call, I go."

As always in life, there was an upside and a downside. Because he was on a 24-hour call, the upside was a beautiful car, and out of necessity, he was allowed to keep the car at his house. The obvious downside was being on a 24-hour call picking up stiffs. Sometimes, during our weekly screw your neighbor card game, he would get a call.

Out of habit, he always asked if one of us wanted to go for a ride. The Buick came equipped with a special collapsible litter, but Dip had no control over what floor the stiff was on, weather, driveway or sidewalk conditions. Therefore, he was always looking for an extra pair of arms and legs. After all Granny's loved ones might find it abrasive if she was accidentally dropped into a storm drain.

One night, I was losing, so I agreed to accompany him on a call. By Dip's standard, the pickup was an easy one, first floor, two-step front porch, light emaciated cadaver, and only two family members at home. We pulled around the back of Salabono's and rolled our cargo onto the special elevator designed for coffins.

The elevator button "dinged" signaling we arrived in the morgue. Dip showed me how to slide our silent friend onto a slanted tile table.

When I asked him about the integral drain at the bottom of the table, he informed me, "After you die, your muscles relax."

"So?" I said.

He continued, "Your body leaks fluids; they have to go somewhere."

"No shit," I uttered.

Grinning at me, he said, "Yeah, shit...death smells." On the next table, an autopsy must have been interrupted because there was no one around.

Dip commented, "The county coroner must be full up; otherwise, he wouldn't be using this facility."

"Where is he?" I asked. "Morticians eat dinner just like everyone else," he answered.

Then, without warning, the clout-in-the-ass began explaining the incision, the awful placement in each red bag, and the order in which the five bags were filled. He rambled on about how they were replaced back into the cadaver before sewing it up. I stared at him, hollering, "What is wrong with you? What are you stupid? Let's get the hell out of here!"

***

On the ride back to the card game, he pulled into a Burger King. "Hold your pickle, grab my weenie, have it your way," and ordered his usual sack of grease. At the clown, he turned and asked, "Do you want fries?"

To which I replied, "Hell no, how can you eat?! What the hell is wrong with you?"

"What do you mean? I just thought you might want some fries," he said.

"Shit no," I told him loudly.

Then he grinned and said, "Okay, now I get it, no fries. Hey, they also serve breakfast. Do you want some eggs?"

The sights and smells I encountered that night helped prepare me for Vietnam a couple of years later.

In addition, I learned brutal reality rule #4: "The dead ones can't hurt you; it's the live bastards you have to look out for." I lost heavily at cards that night, never rode with Dip again, and passed on breakfast the next day.

When it was my turn in the junkyard, "the apple of my eye" was a fifteen-year-old Ford coupe. All the required body parts, doors, hood, fenders, and trunk were still intact. It had a lot of rust and was missing some paint, both minor problems I could easily solve. However, some would consider the missing motor and transmission to be a drawback. Dammit, once again reality bit me in the ass. Rule #1: Life is not fair.

Maybe there is a God because the guys found another Ford on the lot, complete with a usable drive train. One look and it is evident that something large, going very fast, hit the rear of that car. Thankfully, the drive train was in the front and still in good shape. Better yet, we had the combined knowledge and manpower to remove and replace the motor.

There was only one thing left to address. My financial resources were not boundless, and I had to negotiate the purchase of two cars.

I found the pant load sitting in his office, reading porn. I began, "Bernie, today is your lucky day. This is such a deal!" I continued, "I am paying you for two cars but only taking one, in addition, completely free of charge, my expert mechanics will remove a motor from one of your worthless wrecks. You profit twice by selling me one car for cash and still keep the wreck for sale later!"

He looked at me and smiled. As I counted his missing teeth, my heart began sinking. "Show me the two cars," he said. After completing an in-depth inventory, he announced, "Four hundred!"

That lit my board, and I suggested where he could put his motors, cars, office, and the entire lot! He smiled again and said, "Five hundred!"

Skunked, I paid him the five hundred dollars in cash and then froze my ass off for hours pulling two and installing one drive train. We began towing the car, and he trotted off toward the pub. Brutal reality rule #1, "Life's not fair." Brutal reality rule #2, "There is no cure for stupid."

Nursing a bruised ego, I placed a rag in my bleeding ass and started home. I had enough resources left to purchase a gallon of white high gloss Rust-Oleum paint, one paint brush, and enough rope to tie the driver's side door shut. Restoration complete, I stepped back to gaze on my breath-taking piece of mechanical art. It was beautiful, screw Mickey.

Later that week, a county cop gave me my first ticket for "littering the highway." He pulled me over on a beautiful morning. The bright sunshine bouncing off my custom high gloss paint job hurt his eyes. Squinting, he asked, "What the hell is this supposed to be?"

"This is a fully restored Ford coupe," I replied with pride.

"Get this wreck out of here and never drive it on my highway again," he warned. Obviously, the officer was not a student of the arts. As I drove onto the nearest exit, I thought, 'Jealousy is such an ugly emotion.'

***

Three weeks later, it was Luke's turn to visit Bernie's "Rent A Junk Heap" car lot. His taste in transportation was more eclectic, and he settled on a 1953 Ford sedan. The front, rear, and one side were "like new." Unfortunately, the passenger side was stoved in from bumper to bumper. My best guess is a large snow plow hit it, "T boning" the car.

Luke considered it to be an "added value custom feature" and forked over $400. Bernie headed for the pub and we pulled another piece of s--t off his lot.

Within a week after quietly visiting Bernie's lot to acquire some "midnight specials" and cashing in on a few "five-finger discounts," Luke's car was running.

On Sundays, you could find him parked down by the river with the car's good side always facing the road. Bless him, he washed and waxed three-quarters of a car every week.

Chapter Fourteen

FELLOW AMERICANS

*M*oney *isn't everything, but money is far ahead of whatever is in second place. In the 1960s, an 18-year-old had either money or a draft notice. During the Vietnam conflict, when their country was called, most of our current politicians declined to serve. Some were called more than once, but all of them had better things to do than serve their country in its time of need. The result is an abundance of sunshine patriots; ironically, they exude little warmth.*

Remember when our Democracy calls, if you refuse to answer, some-one else must go in your place. Those who could not care less have a right to do so because many fought and died to ensure your rights. -Walter

***

To date, this "unique generation of patriots" still refuses to accept any responsibility for their actions. They consider themselves irreproachable and above judgment (American heroes). They can't have it both ways; either we live in a democracy with government by the people and for the people, or those who refuse to defend our way of life weaken America by their example. Throughout history, the fortunate ones and the Senator's sons have always avoided defending America.

All the guys knew why our classmates were pursuing higher education; a college deferment protected you from being drafted. Starting with President Lincoln, who initiated America's first conscription, those who could afford to buy a deferment were granted one for a fee of $300; you or your loved ones were protected from serving in the Civil War.

Arguably, some people living in the North decided slavery was a better option than fighting to end it. Imitating President Lincoln during the Vietnam conflict, President Johnson and Secretary of Defense Robert Mac Namara provided deferments to anyone who could afford college. None of us could afford the tuition, and as a result, we were drafted in place of the politician's sons and the fortunate ones (great song by Credence Clearwater Revival). A hard lesson in brutal reality, "some of us drink champagne while others die of thirst." Half a century later, my memory of friends who died protecting all Americans brings sadness.

I came home from work, opened the kitchen door, and tried to fathom why my father and brother were beside themselves laughing at me. They pointed to a legal-sized envelope. There, on my dinner plate, stuck into a pile of mashed potatoes was my draft notice. In case you never received one, they start out, "Greetings from the selective service, your friends and neighbors have selected you..." I couldn't appreciate the humor, and no longer hungry, I left.

Now what? One seeks advice at a time like this and I knew my family would not be helpful. So, as always, it was time to ask the guys. Since all of us were close in age, our draft notices fell like rain; they arrived exactly two weeks after our eighteenth birthday. Each of us made our decision and respected the other's choice.

There were not a lot of options: The selective service provided only two weeks to one month's notice prior to the mandated induction date. Therefore, a college or parental (married couples with children) deferment was not viable. Anyone drafted who did not report was subject to imprisonment. Upon release from incarceration, you were still subject to the draft. This was 1966, long before the wizards in the White House initiated a lottery.

One could protest the Vietnam conflict and leave the country.

Drafted, you served two years active duty, two years active reserve, and two years inactive reserve. The idea that you are drafted into the Army is incorrect. You are conscripted into the armed forces.

Once you have taken the oath at induction to defend your country, you are no longer protected by civilian law. You are judged by and subject to the "Uniform Code of Military Justice."

Politicians, your "fellow Americans," can do whatever they want with you. Throughout the Vietnam conflict, the United States Marine Corps filled its ranks with "drafted inductees."

After the oath was administered, the Corps selected its share of available manpower. In my group, they selected every third row, totaling more than just "a few good men," they chose thousands of "good men."

Enlistment in the Army was three years of active duty and three years of inactive duty.

Enlistment in the Navy or Air Force was four years active and two years inactive.

Enlistment in the Coast Guard was for six years of active duty.

I had no way of foreseeing a perfect storm was coming. Bear in mind that this was 1966. President Johnson was not "elected," he simply succeeded President Kennedy after the assassination. Johnson inherited Kennedy's Secretary of Defense, Mr. Robert Strange (yes Strange) Mac Namara. Before being appointed Secretary of Defense by President Kennedy, he toiled as one of Ford Motor Company's "Whiz Kids" (Whiz Kid is Ford's definition, not mine).

President Johnson and Mac Namara informed the country that American Naval destroyers were attacked in international waters (on two separate occasions) by North Vietnam. I had no way of knowing the story was a "fairy tale" at the time; no one else did either. The President went to Congress (the American people) and received permission to start a "conflict" in Vietnam. Refer to "In Retrospect: The Tragedy and Lessons of Vietnam," written by Robert S. Mac Namara. A quote from Mr. Mac Namara: "We were wrong, terribly wrong. We owe it to future generations to explain why."

I should have been more diligent. Korean veterans were still trying to decipher how a "police action" killed 36,000 of their friends and family members. America's invasion of Korea was an unauthorized military action by President Truman, with approval from the Congress and the Senate. The term "police action," instead of "war," provided them a convenient way to disregard Article 1, Section 8 of our Constitution.

Congress (the American people) incurs responsibilities when a formal declaration of war is made. America becomes responsible for the dead and wounded military personnel it sent into harm's way. By utilizing wistful synonyms such as "police action" and "conflict," politicians secured a measure of freedom from the tremendous cost of undeclared military actions. Some veteran benefits guaranteed to <u>war</u> veterans via the Constitution could be delayed or discounted, thereby minimizing tax increases and enhancing reelection. Elected officials deemed their actions to be of little consequence since only a small percentage of them would ever see combat anywhere.

In 1973, both the Congress and Senate, suffering from mental irregularity, passed the "War Powers Resolution." They bestowed upon the President the power to act alone when ordering military action against a sovereign nation. He could bomb, invade, and occupy a nation without warning, a declaration of war, or the consent of the American people. Apparently, our "pillars of freedom" forgot that in 1941, Japan also bombed a sovereign nation without warning or a declaration of war. Their decision turned into a circle jerk, and Japan wound up getting its tit in a wringer.

Realizing they had some time left before lunch, our leaders included a few provisions; the President must notify Congress of his actions within 48 hours. That gave our statesmen time to trickle back into Washington, DC, after their weekend break.

In addition, they decreed America's invasion force could not occupy an impermanent nation for more than 60 days, plus an additional 30 days to allow for the orderly withdrawal of our troops.

William Jefferson Clinton was the first President to exploit the resolution. It was rumored that his pharmacy had run out of stool softener, and as his need for relief grew, the President fell into a foul mood. Extremely agitated and looking for a way to vent, he opted to bomb the U.S.-chartered, self-declared independent nation of Kosovo.

Congress disapproved, but legal action taken against the President for "alleged violations" was unsuccessful. The legality of bombing innocent citizens in sovereign nations had to be addressed. Alas, it was not to be; in 2000, the Supreme Court disregarded the human consequences and refused to hear the Yugoslavian case. The court abandoned its responsibility to protect the Constitution (They missed the footnote in small print about why only Congress can declare War.) and scurried down a rabbit hole already full of Congressmen.

Confident the court would turn a blind eye, President Clinton occupied Kosovo well beyond the 60-day limit. Presidents Kennedy (Vietnam), Johnson Vietnam/ Laos/ Cambodia), Nixon (Vietnam), Reagan (El Salvador), and Obama (Libya) have flexed their power. Most of them paid little heed to the restrictions Congress included in the resolution.

For example, President Johnson neglected to inform Congress about bombing Cambodia. Big deal he forgot; besides, he was certain the Supreme Court, Congress, and Senate would look the other way as they had so many times before.

Indeed, several American Presidents, along with the Senate and Congress, acted well outside of the Constitution. The executive and legislative branches of government went rogue. Congress (you) supported an "undeclared war" in Vietnam by referring to it as a "conflict." Then Congress voted "ad nauseam" to continue funding that "conflict" for a decade. Vietnam was the first time Americans in combat were televised, and the President, Senators, and Congressmen watched nightly as the reality show they created unfolded endlessly. Biased news reporters were embedded with the troops, ensuring all political parties an equal chance to "win over the hearts of the American people."

Imagine their surprise when the American people could no longer condone what was being done in their name. Enough was enough; someone had to pay for the nation's bad behavior. For reasons that still defy logic, "that someone was the Vietnam veteran." Veterans, not politicians, were held accountable by the nation, the same nation that sent him or her to Vietnam, considered guilty for all the unconstitutional malfeasance they were criminalized and victimized by their government and media for decades. If they survived and returned home, draft dodgers, protestors, and deserters "joined in", determined to make everyday life difficult for the Vietnam veteran and his family. Never or since has a generation (the baby boomers) of Americans vilified their Army instead of its politicians for the consequences of war (conflict). The President, Congress, and Senate stood by refusing to assist the same veterans they sent to war. Correction, the same veterans they conscripted to settle a "conflict."

***

I decided to start with Larry first. You would have liked the guy. He was quick to smile, full of life, and never took himself seriously. His dad was gone, and his mother was a prototype for all the single moms to come. Larry decided to go with the draft and eventually wound up in Vietnam. Trained as a machine gunner, he served with a light infantry brigade on the DMZ between North and South Vietnam.

At the request of his fellow Americans, every night for one year, he did his job, finding, killing, and wounding North Vietnamese soldiers. He fought for "fellow Americans" who would criminalize him upon his return. They would also delay and/or deny his veteran benefits.

One day, something blew up near Larry. What blew up, we will never know. The post-Vietnam Larry came home without his short-term memory and most of his hearing. However, he did bring home a violent case of PTSD and a love of alcohol.

Larry and I walked over to Rob's house, an easy-going guy, trusting and very religious. He lost his mother before he turned nine. By default, while still in grade school, he became his younger sister's main caretaker. Rob's father had to work six days a week, and there were no resources for professional assistance. Rob's sister was slowly dying of multiple sclerosis, and before leaving for school, he would clean, feed, and prepare her for the day. Then go home immediately after school to begin the process anew. The guys would drift over most afternoons to place Elizabeth on a blanket in the living room. Lying on her back, she would kick and smile while we played guitar and sang to her.

Rob decided he would not be drafted. He had the benefit of counsel, with a loving father and older brother. He elected to join the Navy. His specialty would be airplane electronics. By taking this approach, he reasoned he would be safe from harm. After training, Rob sailed on an aircraft carrier on an oblong course 280 miles off the coast of Vietnam for three years.

He did his best, and on some tours, he served as a plane captain. Rob had no way of knowing that his jet was escorting tankers that dropped Agent Blue and Agent Orange. Before returning to the Carrier, covered in toxins, the jet would sortie in and out of Da Nang Air Base. Rob cleaned and repaired these Navy jets for years. As a result, he died slowly from cancer (stage four melanoma) caused by three years of heavy exposure to Agent Orange.

After four years of decorated service, Rob was separated from active duty. His "fellow Americans" and their democratically elected politicians took note. Just as they did with Larry, they made sure to criminalize him. He, too, was considered a murderer and baby killer.

The next day, I drove over to visit Pip in the neighboring town. A quiet guy, Pip was older than his sister and a part of a great family. His dad was awarded both a Bronze Star and a Purple Heart during WWII. Pip was going into the draft and would eventually wind up in the IA Drang Valley with the First Air Cavalry. One day, the NVA shelled and hit his bunker... twice! First to hit was a mortar round followed by a rocket. He came home without 85 percent of his hearing, and in soft speak, he brought with him some issues. Issues stemming, in part, from shrapnel wounds received on two previous engagements.

After returning home, the guys visited him often and worked with him for almost a year. It took that long to get him to leave his room. Since he would not seek employment, showed no sign of getting better, and the family physician was unable to help, we took him to the local VA hospital. I was in the eligibility office when the VA fired up their computer and informed him that he was never in Vietnam. In addition, they had no record of his receiving two Purple Hearts. When he acquired proper documentation, they would consider a rating higher than his current 8. Naturally, it was entirely his responsibility, certainly not theirs, even though they had all the records, to prove he was a combat veteran. The damage done that morning almost took Pip back to square one.

The guys spent about six months straightening out his records utilizing a lot of forms, telephone hours, letters, and certified mail. One item on his medical record was noteworthy. Pip failed his hearing test at his initial induction physical. Even though he was hearing impaired, his "fellow Americans" drafted him into active military service. Even more bizarre, the army assigned him to an artillery unit in Vietnam, and at his separation physical, he was deemed by them to have perfect hearing! Groundbreaking medical discovery, the cure for loss of hearing is to fire a 105MM howitzer for two years!

The VA finally agreed to a hearing exam, and once again, they told Pip he had perfect hearing. Imagine his surprise when they issued him a pair of hearing aids!? He began to self-medicate and alcoholism followed. After serving his country in time of "conflict," he spent his life deaf and drunk. Nobody, nobody gave a shit. Not one of his "fellow Americans."

Mickey was my next stop. His was a close family, complete with a devoutly religious mother, older brother, and loving father. They had discussed the draft in depth, and Mickey was enlisting. The safe bet was to become a Russian translator for the United States Air Force. I have little doubt that Mickey was a great translator. However, what the Air Force neglected to mention to him during enlistment was that he would be buried three times under the ice in Greenland. Mickey was ordered to help a man at a listening post close to the Russian border. Due to severe weather, his base would be isolated for months. He was buried alive on three separate occasions for several months at a time.

I assume the Navy screens submariners. Apparently, the Air Force does not screen Russian interpreters before burial. Each year the appearance and behavior changes in Mickey were pronounced. When his active service was over, he purchased a motorcycle, married a pole dancer, and blew his brains out a decade later. Mickey never asked his "fellow Americans," including those who protested, deserted, and declined to serve for a damn thing.

Luke's mother answered my knock. She explained he was in Connecticut, living with her sister. His aunt had entered Luke into the summer program and would foot the bill for four years of college. Since he was going to college full-time, the draft board could not touch him. I never met Luke's aunt, but I love her for saving him. Upon his return, degree in hand, he married his childhood sweetheart. Luke had a long career teaching mathematics in a local high school. Maybe there is a God.

My last stop was at Dip's house. His nickname stemmed from a road sign in front of his home alerting oncoming motorists to a dip in the road. After several discussions with family members, Dip decided he would enlist in the Navy and make it known he was a "conscientious objector." The Navy accepted him and trained him as a medic.

It turns out the Marines, who just happened to be in Vietnam, used Navy corpsmen. The Marines got another good man. He got what he wanted, sort of, since he was not armed. After grave registration, being a medic was a gruesome and brutal row to hoe in a combat zone. The family moved during his four-year tour, so I never found out what happened to Dip.

Armed with all the input I was going to get, I made the decision to be drafted. As a draftee, I had no say in where I was sent or what I did. I would spend my tour in Vietnam assigned to an AWSP battalion. AWSP was the Army's abbreviation for Automatic Weapons Self-Propelled. The battalion was comprised of 50 caliber machine guns, quad-mounted on armor-plated trucks, twin 40 MM cannons, tub-mounted on a light tank chassis, and infrared searchlights mounted on jeeps.

Along with Rob, Larry, and Pip, I live with health conditions resulting from my exposure to Agent Orange. Aside from PTSD, a blood disorder, and neuropathy, tinnitus, and a bum thyroid, I rely on hearing aids and a pacemaker.

Looking back on my bouncy ride through life, I consider myself to be blessed. America is a great country, and I have confidence that younger generations will only add to its greatness (my generation, not so much). My family, unconventional at best, provided rock-solid support and a lifetime full of pleasant memories.

Go figure.

Epilogue

"So, what do you think doc? Do you think any of this makes a difference? Do you actually think someone is going to read this?
"Yes, Walter, I do."

***

The Therapist's Final Remarks:

***

If you have stayed around until now, you are probably wondering, "So what happened to Walter? Where is he now?"

***

At the present moment (2021), Walter is 74 years old. He is married to an incredible woman who has remained at his side for 51 years. They have two children and four grandchildren. Walter possesses a deep sense of love and pride for his family. He often shares photos and stories about the grandkids, bragging about their accomplishments. It is not surprising that after experiencing a great deal of trauma and loss in his lifetime, Walter is fiercely protective of those closest to him. Walter is still in weekly therapy and exercises regularly with his trainer, who he jokingly refers to as "grumpy." He no longer requires the use of a cane, has lost 70 pounds, and recently had his diabetes diagnosis removed.

I am in awe, recalling his journey and progress over the last 14 months. In my opinion, Walter is one of the lucky ones. He has always stuck to the lessons learned through "brutal reality" and I believe he survived, in large part because of these early teachings. There have been many more men and women who can't be here to tell their story. In part, this book also pays tribute to those lost. They will not be forgotten, and I thank them for their service.

I owe Walter a tremendous amount of gratitude. His dedication and motivation to change the relationship to his circumstances are inspiring. In writing his story, he said "if I can help one person, just one, this will have all been worth it." Well Walter, you have already helped one person and my guess is many more. Thank you for you honest candor and for keeping the door open to human kindness.
-Christina Romeo

***

One final word of advice: NEVER ask a Vietnam veteran, "Why are you still so angry?"

***

THE END